Buffalo Gals

And Other Animal Presences

---

by Ursula K. Le Guin

Illustrated by
Margaret Chodos-Irvine

A ROC BOOK

ROC
Published by the Penguin Group
Penguin Books USA Inc., 375 Hudson Street, New York, New York 10014, U.S.A.
Penguin Books Ltd, 27 Wrights Lane, London W8 5TZ, England
Penguin Books Australia Ltd, Ringwood, Victoria, Australia
Penguin Books Canada Ltd, 10 Alcorn Avenue, Toronto, Ontario, Canada M4V 3B2
Penguin Books (N.Z.) Ltd, 182–190 Wairau Road, Auckland 10, New Zealand

Penguin Books Ltd, Registered Offices:
Harmondsworth, Middlesex, England

Published by Roc, an imprint of Dutton Signet, a division of Penguin Books USA Inc. This is an
authorized reprint of a hardcover edition published by Capra Press. *Buffalo Gals* also previously
appeared in Plume and Roc mass market editions.

First Roc Trade Paperback Printing, December, 1994
10 9 8 7 6 5 4 3 2 1

ACKNOWLEDGEMENTS
"Come Into Animal Presences" Denise Levertov, Poems 1960–1967, © 1961 by Denise Levertov
Goodman; reprinted by permission of New Directions Publishing Corporation. Excerpt from
"Original Sin" © 1948 by Robinson Jeffers; reprinted from *Selected Poems* by permission of
Random House, Inc. "Elegy" by Rainer Maria Rilke is the translation of Ursula K. Le Guin.
"Buffalo Gals, Won't You Come Out Tonight" © 1987 by Ursula K. Le Guin; first appeared in *The
Magazine of Fantasy and Science Fiction* Nov. 1987. "The Basalt" © 1982 by Ursula K. Le Guin;
first appeared in *Open Places 33* Spring 1982. "Mount St. Helens/Omphalos" © 1975 by Ursula
K. Le Guin; first appeared in *Wild Angels* by Ursula K. Le Guin, Capra Press, 1975. "The Wife's
Story" © 1982 by Ursula K. Le Guin; first appeared in *Compass Rose* by Ursula K. Le Guin,
Harper & Row, 1982. "Mazes" © 1975 by Ursula K. Le Guin; first appeared in *Epoch*, edited by
Robert Silverberg and Roger Elwood. "Torrey Pines Reserve" © 1981 by Ursula K. Le Guin; first
appeared in *Hard Words* by Ursula K. Le Guin, Harper & Row, 1981. "Lewis and Clark and After"
© 1987 by Ursula K. Le Guin; first appeared in *The Seattle Review,* Summer 1987. "Xmas Over"
© 1984 by Ursula K. Le Guin; first appeared in *Clinton Street Quarterly,* 1984. "The Direction
of the Road" © 1974 by Ursula K. Le Guin; first appeared in *Orbit 14*, edited by Damon Knight.
"Vaster Than Empires and More Slow" © 1971 by Ursula K. Le Guin; first appeared in *New
Directions 1*, edited by Robert Silverberg. "For Ted" © 1975 by Ursula K. Le Guin; first appeared
in *Wild Angels* by Ursula K. Le Guin, Capra Press, 1975. "Totem" © 1981 by Ursula
K. Le Guin; first appeared in *Hard Words* by Ursula K. Le Guin, Harper & Row, 1981. "Winter
Downs" © 1981 by Ursula K. Le Guin; first appeared in *Hard Words* by Ursula K. Le Guin,
Harper & Row, 1981. "The White Donkey" © 1980 by Ursula K. Le Guin; first appeared in
TriQuarterly, Fall 1980. "Horse Camp" © 1986 by Ursula K. Le Guin; first appeared in *The New
Yorker,* August 25, 1986. "Shrödinger's Cat" © 1974 by Ursula K. Le Guin; first appeared in
Universe 5, edited by Terry Carr. "The Author of the Acacia Seeds and Other Extracts From the
Journal of the Association of Therolinguistics" © 1974 by Ursula K. Le Guin; first appeared in
Fellowship of the Stars, edited by Terry Carr. "May's Lion" © 1983 by Ursula K. Le Guin; first
appeared in *The Little Magazine*. Volume 14, combined Numbers 1 & 2. "She Unnames Them"
© 1985 by Ursula K. Le Guin; first appeared in *The New Yorker,* January 21, 1985.

RoC REGISTERED TRADEMARK—MARCA REGISTRADA

The Library of Congress has cataloged the Plume edition as follows:
Library of Congress Cataloging-in-Publication

Le Guin, Ursula K., 1929–
    Buffalo gals and other animal presences / by Ursula K. Le Guin.
        p.   cm.
    ISBN 0-452-26480-4
    ISBN 0-451-45434-0 (Roc Trade Paperback)
    I. Animals—Literary collections.   Title.
[PS3562.E42B8   1988]   88-15583
813′.54—dc19   CIP
Printed in the United States of America

BOOKS BY URSULA K. LE GUIN

Contents

Buffalo Gals

Introduction

ALTHOUGH I WHINED and tried to hide under the rug, my inexorable publisher demanded an introduction for this book of my stories and poems about animals. Having done introductions before, I have found that many readers loathe them, reviewers sneer at them, and critics dismiss them; and then they all tell me so. As for myself I rather like introductions, but generally read them after reading what they were supposed to introduce me to. Read as extra-ductions, they are often interesting and useful. But that won't do. Ductions must be intro, and come first, like salad in restaurants, a lot of cardboard lettuce with bits of red wooden cabbage soaked in dressing, so that you're disabled for the entree.

The kind of introduction that comes naturally is oral. Reading aloud to an audience, one often talks a little about what one is going to read; and so for each section of this book I have tried to write down the kind of thing I might say about the pieces if I were performing them.

As for the book as a whole: first of all I am grateful to my inexorable publisher for having the idea of doing such a collection, and for asking me to write a long new story for it. It was his request that gave me the story "Buffalo Gals." Three other stories have not been printed in book form before, and twelve of the poems have not been printed anywhere till now. They are not all exactly about animals. In fact this is a sort of Twenty Questions anthology—

animal, vegetable, or mineral? But the animals, naturally, are more active. And more talkative.

What about talking animals, anyhow?

In his literary biography of Rudyard Kipling, so sympathetic and perceptive a reader/writer as Angus Wilson dismisses the *Jungle Books* as schoolboy stories with animal costumes, and has no truck at all with the *Just So Stories.* As I think the *Jungle Books,* along with the other "children's story," *Kim,* are Kipling's finest work, and consider the *Just So Stories* a unique and miraculous interaction of prose with poetry with graphics, of adult mind with child mind, and of written with oral literature—a shining intersection among endless dreary one-way streets—so Wilson's dismissal of them was something I needed to understand. Not that it was anything unusual. Critical terror of Kiddilit is common. People to whom sophistication is a positive intellectual value shun anything "written for children"; if you want to clear the room of derrideans, mention Beatrix Potter without sneering. With the agreed exception of *Alice in Wonderland,* books for children are to be mentioned only dismissively or jocosely by the adult male critic. Just as Angus Wilson used to dismiss Virginia Woolf uncomfortably, jocosely, as a lady novelist, though he finally and creditably admitted that he might have missed something there ... In literature as in "real life," women, children, and animals are the obscure matter upon which Civilization erects itself, phallologically. That they are Other is (*vide* Lacan *et al.*) the foundation of language, the Father Tongue. If Man vs. Nature is the name of the game, no wonder the team players kick out all these non-men who won't learn the rules and run around the cricket pitch squeaking and barking and chattering!

But then, who are the Bandar-Log?

Why do animals in kids' books talk? Why do animals in myths talk? How come the prince eats a burned fish-scale and all of a sudden understands what the mice in the wall are saying about the kingdom? How come on Christmas night the beasts in the stables speak to one another in human voices? Why does the tortoise say, "I'll race you," to the hare, and how does Coyote tell Death, "I'll do exactly what you tell me!" Animals don't talk—everybody knows that. Everybody, including quite small children, and the men and women who told and tell talking-animal stories, knows that animals are dumb: have no words of their own. So why do we keep putting words into their mouths?

We who? We the dumb: the others.

In the dreadful self-isolation of the Church, that soul-fortress towering over the dark abysms of the bestial/mortal/World/Hell, for St. Francis to cry out "Sister sparrow, brother wolf!" was a great thing. But for the Buddha to be a jackal or a monkey was no big deal. And for the people Civilization calls "primitive," "savage," or "undeveloped," including young children, the continuity, interdependence, and community of all life, all forms of being on earth, is a lived fact, made conscious in narrative (myth, ritual, fiction). This continuity of existence, neither benevolent nor cruel itself, is fundamental to whatever morality may be built upon it. Only Civilization builds its morality by denying its foundation.

By climbing up into his head and shutting out every voice but his own, "Civilized Man" has gone deaf. He can't hear the wolf calling him brother—not Master, but brother. He can't hear the earth calling him child—not Father, but son. He hears only his own words making up the world. He can't hear the animals, they have nothing to say. Children babble, and have to be taught how to climb up into their heads and shut the doors of perception. No use teaching women at all, they talk all the time, of course, but never say anything. This is the myth of Civilization, embodied in the monotheisms which assign soul to Man alone.

And so it is this myth which all talking-animal stories mock, or simply subvert. So long as "man" "rules," animals will make rude remarks about him. Women and unruly men will tell their daughters and sons what the fox said to the ox, what Raven told South Wind. And the cat will say, "I am the Cat that walks by himself, and all places are alike to me!" And the Man, infuriated by this failure to acknowledge Hierarchy, will throw his boots and his little stone ax (that makes three) at the Cat. Only when the Man listens, and attends, O Best Beloved, and hears, and understands, will the Cat return to the Cat's true silence.

When the word is not sword, but shuttle.

But still there will be stories, there will always be stories, in which the lion's mother scolds the lion, and the fish cries out to the fisherman, and the cat talks; because it is true that all creatures talk to one another, if only one listens.

This conversation, this community, is not a simple harmony. The Peaceable Kingdom, where lion and lamb lie down, is an endearing vision not of this world. It denies wilderness. And voices cry in the wilderness.

Users of words to get outside the head with, rash poets get caught in the traps set for animals. Some, unable to endure the cruelty, maim themselves to escape. Robinson Jeffers's "Original Sin" describes the "happy hunters" of the Stone Age, puzzled how to kill the mammoth trapped in their pitfall, discovering that they can do so by building fires around it and roasting it alive all day. The poem ends:

> I would rather
> Be a worm in a wild apple than a son of man.
> But we are what we are, and we might remember
> Not to hate any person, for all are vicious;
> And not to be astonished at any evil, all are deserved;
> And not to fear death; it is the only way to be cleansed.

This may be wrongheaded, but I prefer it to the generous but sloppy identifications of Walt Whitman. Where Whitman takes the animal into his vast, intensely civilized ego, possesses it, engulfs and annihilates it, Jeffers at least reaches out and touches the animal, the Other, through pain, and releases it. But the touching hand is crippled. Perhaps it is only when the otherness, the difference, the space between us (in which both cruelty and love occur) is perceived as holy ground, as the sacred place, that we can "come into animal presence"—the title of Denise Levertov's poem, which honors my book, and stands here as its true introduction.

Come into Animal Presence

Come into animal presence.
No man is so guileless as
the serpent. The lonely white
rabbit on the roof is a star
twitching its ears at the rain.
The llama intricately
folding its hind legs to be seated
not disdains but mildly
disregards human approval.
What joy when the insouciant
armadillo glances at us and doesn't
quicken his trotting
across the track into the palm bush.
What is this joy? That no animal
falters, but knows what it must do?
That the snake has no blemish,
that the rabbit inspects his strange surroundings
in white star-silence? The llama
rests in dignity, the armadillo
has some intention to pursue in the palm forest.
Those who were sacred have remained so,
holiness does not dissolve, it is a presence
of bronze, only the sight that saw it
faltered and turned from it.
An old joy returns in holy presence.

—DENISE LEVERTOV

I

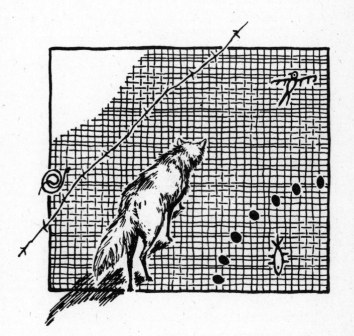

Buffalo Gals,
Won't You Come Out Tonight

"YOU FELL OUT OF THE SKY," the coyote said.

Still curled up tight, lying on her side, her back pressed against the overhanging rock, the child watched the coyote with one eye. Over the other eye she kept her hand cupped, its back on the dirt.

"There was a burned place in the sky, up there alongside the rimrock, and then you fell out of it," the coyote repeated, patiently, as if the news was getting a bit stale. "Are you hurt?"

She was all right. She was in the plane with Mr. Michaels, and the motor was so loud she couldn't understand what he said even when he shouted, and the way the wind rocked the wings was making her feel sick, but it was all right. They were flying to Canyonville. In the plane.

She looked. The coyote was still sitting there. It yawned. It was a big one, in good condition, its coat silvery and thick. The dark tear-line from its long yellow eye was as clearly marked as a tabby cat's.

She sat up, slowly, still holding her right hand pressed to her right eye.

"Did you lose an eye?" the coyote asked, interested.

"I don't know," the child said. She caught her breath and shivered. "I'm cold."

"I'll help you look for it," the coyote said. "Come on! If you move around you won't have to shiver. The sun's up."

Cold lonely brightness lay across the falling land, a hundred miles of sagebrush. The coyote was trotting busily around, nosing under clumps of rabbit-brush and cheatgrass, pawing at a rock. "Aren't you going to look?" it said, suddenly sitting down on its haunches and abandoning the search. "I knew a trick once where I could throw my eyes way up into a tree and see everything from up there, and then whistle, and they'd come back into my head. But that goddam bluejay stole them, and when I whistled nothing came. I had to stick lumps of pine pitch into my head so I could see anything. You could try that. But you've got one eye that's OK, what do you need two for? Are you coming, or are you dying there?"

The child crouched, shivering.

"Well, come if you want to," said the coyote, yawned again, snapped at a flea, stood up, turned, and trotted away among the sparse clumps of rabbit-brush and sage, along the long slope that stretched on down and down into the plain streaked across by long shadows of sagebrush. The slender, grey-yellow animal was hard to keep in sight, vanishing as the child watched.

She struggled to her feet, and without a word, though she kept saying in her mind, "Wait, please wait," she hobbled after the coyote. She could not see it. She kept her hand pressed over the right eyesocket. Seeing with one eye there was no depth; it was like a huge, flat picture. The coyote suddenly sat in the middle of the picture, looking back at her, its mouth open, its eyes narrowed, grinning. Her legs began to steady and her head did not pound so hard, though the deep, black ache was always there. She had nearly caught up to the coyote when it trotted off again. This time she spoke. "Please wait!" she said.

"OK," said the coyote, but it trotted right on. She

followed, walking downhill into the flat picture that at each step was deep.

Each step was different underfoot; each sage bush was different, and all the same. Following the coyote she came out from the shadow of the rimrock cliffs, and the sun at eyelevel dazzled her left eye. Its bright warmth soaked into her muscles and bones at once. The air, that all night had been so hard to breathe, came sweet and easy.

The sage bushes were pulling in their shadows and the sun was hot on the child's back when she followed the coyote along the rim of a gully. After a while the coyote slanted down the undercut slope and the child scrambled after, through scrub willows to the thin creek in its wide sandbed. Both drank.

The coyote crossed the creek, not with a careless charge and splashing like a dog, but singlefoot and quiet like a cat; always it carried its tail low. The child hesitated, knowing that wet shoes make blistered feet, and then waded across in as few steps as possible. Her right arm ached with the effort of holding her hand up over her eye. "I need a bandage," she said to the coyote. It cocked its head and said nothing. It stretched out its forelegs and lay watching the water, resting but alert. The child sat down nearby on the hot sand and tried to move her right hand. It was glued to the skin around her eye by dried blood. At the little tearing-away pain, she whimpered; though it was a small pain it frightened her. The coyote came over close and poked its long snout into her face. Its strong, sharp smell was in her nostrils. It began to lick the awful, aching blindness, cleaning and cleaning with its curled, precise, strong, wet tongue, until the child was able to cry a little with relief, being comforted. Her head was bent close to the grey-yellow ribs, and she saw the hard nipples, the whitish belly-fur. She put her arm around the she-coyote, stroking the harsh coat over back and ribs.

"OK," the coyote said, "let's go!" And set off without a backward glance. The child scrambled to her feet and followed. "Where are we going?" she said, and the coyote, trotting on down along the creek, answered, "On down along the creek..."

There must have been a while she was asleep while she walked, because she felt like she was waking up, but she was walking along, only in a different place. She didn't know how she knew it was different. They were still following the creek, though the gully was flattened out to nothing much, and there was still sagebrush range as far as the eye could see. The eye—the good one—felt rested. The other one still ached, but not so sharply, and there was no use thinking about it. But where was the coyote?

She stopped. The pit of cold into which the plane had fallen re-opened and she fell. She stood falling, a thin whimper making itself in her throat.

"Over here!"

The child turned. She saw a coyote gnawing at the half-dried-up carcass of a crow, black feathers sticking to the black lips and narrow jaw.

She saw a tawny-skinned woman kneeling by a campfire, sprinkling something into a conical pot. She heard the water boiling in the pot, though it was propped between rocks, off the fire. The woman's hair was yellow and grey, bound back with a string. Her feet were bare. The upturned soles looked as dark and hard as shoe soles, but the arch of the foot was high, and the toes made two neat curving rows. She wore bluejeans and an old white shirt. She looked over at the girl. "Come on, eat crow!" she said. The child slowly came toward the woman and the fire, and squatted down. She had stopped falling and felt very light and empty; and her tongue was like a piece of wood stuck in her mouth.

Coyote was now blowing into the pot or basket or whatever it was. She reached into it with two fingers, and pulled her hand away shaking it and shouting, "Ow! Shit! Why don't I ever have any spoons?" She broke off a dead twig of sagebrush, dipped it into the pot, and licked it. "Oh, boy," she said. "Come on!"

The child moved a little closer, broke off a twig, dipped. Lumpy pinkish mush clung to the twig. She licked. The taste was rich and delicate.

"What is it?" she asked after a long time of dipping and licking.

"Food. Dried salmon mush," Coyote said. "It's cooling down." She stuck two fingers into the mush again, this time getting a good load, which she ate very neatly. The child, when she tried, got mush all over her chin. It was like chopsticks, it took practice. She practiced. They ate turn and turn until nothing was left in the pot but three rocks. The child did not ask why there were rocks in the mush-pot. They licked the rocks clean. Coyote licked out the inside of the pot-basket, rinsed it once in the creek, and put it onto her head. It fit nicely, making a conical hat. She pulled off her bluejeans. "Piss on the fire!" she cried, and did so, standing straddling it. "Ah, steam between the legs!" she said. The child, embarrassed, thought she was supposed to do the same thing, but did not want to, and did not. Bareassed, Coyote danced around the dampened fire, kicking her long thin legs out and singing,

> "Buffalo gals, won't you come out tonight,
> Come out tonight, come out tonight,
> Buffalo gals, won't you come out tonight,
> And dance by the light of the moon?"

She pulled her jeans back on. The child was burying the remains of the fire in creek-sand, heaping it over, seriously, wanting to do right. Coyote watched her.

"Is that you?" she said. "A Buffalo Gal? What happened to the rest of you?"

"The rest of me?" The child looked at herself, alarmed.

"All your people."

"Oh. Well, Mom took Bobbie, he's my little brother, away with Uncle Norm. He isn't really my uncle, or anything. So Mr. Michaels was going there anyway so he was going to fly me over to my real father, in Canyonville. Linda, my stepmother, you know, she said it was OK for the summer anyhow if I was there, and then we could see. But the plane."

In the silence the girl's face became dark red, then greyish white. Coyote watched, fascinated. "Oh," the girl said, "Oh—Oh—Mr. Michaels—he must be—Did the—"

"Come on!" said Coyote, and set off walking.

The child cried, "I ought to go back —"

"What for?" said Coyote. She stopped to look round at the child, then went on faster. "Come on, Gal!" She said it as a name; maybe it was the child's name, Myra, as spoken by Coyote. The child, confused and despairing, protested again, but followed her. "Where are we going? Where *are* we?"

"This is my country," Coyote answered, with dignity, making a long, slow gesture all round the vast horizon. "I made it. Every goddam sage bush."

And they went on. Coyote's gait was easy, even a little shambling, but she covered the ground; the child struggled not to drop behind. Shadows were beginning to pull themselves out again from under the rocks and shrubs. Leaving the creek, they went up a long, low, uneven slope that ended away off against the sky in rimrock. Dark trees stood one here, another way over there; what people called a juniper forest, a desert forest, one with a lot more between the trees than trees. Each juniper they passed smelled sharply, cat-pee smell the kids at school called it, but the child liked it; it seemed to go into her mind and wake her up. She picked off a juniper berry and held it in her mouth, but after a while spat it out. The aching was coming back in huge black waves, and she kept stumbling. She found that she was sitting down on the ground. When she tried to get up her legs shook and would not go under her. She felt foolish and frightened, and began to cry.

"We're home!" Coyote called from way on up the hill.

The child looked with her one weeping eye, and saw sagebrush, juniper, cheatgrass, rimrock. She heard a coyote yip far off in the dry twilight.

She saw a little town up under the rimrock, board houses, shacks, all unpainted. She heard Coyote call again, "Come on, pup! Come on, Gal, we're home!" She could not get up, so she tried to go on all fours, the long way up the slope to the houses under the rimrock. Long before she got there, several people came to meet her. They were all children, she thought at first, and then began to understand that most of them were grown people, but all were very short; they were broad-bodied, fat, with fine, delicate hands and feet. Their eyes were bright. Some of the women helped her stand up and walk, coaxing her, "It isn't much farther, you're doing fine." In the late dusk lights shone yellow-bright through doorways and through unchinked cracks between boards. Woodsmoke hung sweet in the quiet air. The short people talked and laughed all the time, softly. "Where's she going to stay?"—"Put her in with Robin, they're all asleep already!"—"Oh, she can stay with us."

The child asked hoarsely, "Where's Coyote?"

"Out hunting," the short people said.

A deeper voice spoke: "Somebody new has come into town?"

"Yes, a new person," one of the short men answered.

Among these people the deep-voiced man bulked impressive; he was broad and tall, with powerful hands, a big head, a short neck. They made way for him respectfully. He moved very quietly, respectful of them also. His eyes when he stared down at the child were amazing. When he blinked, it was like the passing of a hand before a candle-flame.

"It's only an owlet," he said. "What have you let happen to your eye, new person?"

"I was—We were flying—"

"You're too young to fly," the big man said in his deep, soft voice. "Who brought you here?"

"Coyote."

And one of the short people confirmed: "She came here with Coyote, Young Owl."

"Then maybe she should stay in Coyote's house tonight," the big man said.

"It's all bones and lonely in there," said a short woman with fat cheeks and a striped shirt. "She can come with us."

That seemed to decide it. The fat-cheeked woman patted the child's arm and took her past several shacks and shanties to a low, windowless house. The doorway was so low even the child had to duck down to enter. There were a lot of people inside, some already there and some crowding in after the fat-cheeked woman. Several babies were fast asleep in cradle-boxes in corners. There was a good fire, and a good smell, like toasted sesame seeds. The child was given food, and ate a little, but her head swam and the blackness in her right eye kept coming across her left eye so she could not see at all for a while. Nobody asked her name or told her what to call them. She heard the children call the fat-cheeked woman Chipmunk. She got up courage finally to say, "Is there somewhere I can go to sleep, Mrs. Chipmunk?"

"Sure, come on," one of the daughters said, "in here," and took the child into a back room, not completely partitioned off from the crowded front room, but dark and uncrowded. Big shelves with mattresses and blankets lined the walls. "Crawl in!" said Chipmunk's daughter, patting the child's arm in the comforting way they had. The child climbed onto a shelf, under a blanket. She laid down her head. She thought, "I didn't brush my teeth."

ii

She woke; she slept again. In Chipmunk's sleeping room it was always stuffy, warm, and half-dark, day and night. People came in and slept and got up and left, night and day. She dozed and slept, got down to drink from the bucket and dipper in the front room, and went back to sleep and doze.

She was sitting up on the shelf, her feet dangling, not feeling bad any more, but dreamy, weak. She felt in her jeans pockets. In the left front one was a pocket comb and a bubblegum wrapper, in the right front, two dollar bills and a quarter and a dime.

Chipmunk and another woman, a very pretty dark-eyed plump one, came in. "So you woke up for your dance!" Chipmunk greeted her, laughing, and sat down by her with an arm around her.

"Jay's giving you a dance," the dark woman said. "He's going to make you all right. Let's get you all ready!"

There was a spring up under the rimrock, that flattened out into a pool with slimy, reedy shores. A flock of noisy children splashing in it ran off and left the child and the two women to bathe. The water was warm on the surface, cold down on the feet and legs. All naked, the two soft-voiced laughing women, their round bellies and breasts, broad hips and buttocks gleaming warm in the late afternoon light, sluiced the child down, washed and stroked her limbs and hands and hair, cleaned around the cheekbone and eyebrow of her right eye with infinite softness, admired her, sudsed her, rinsed her, splashed her out of the water, dried her off, dried each other off, got dressed, dressed her, braided her hair, braided each other's hair, tied feathers on the braid-ends, admired her and each other again, and brought her back down into the little straggling town and to a kind of playing field or dirt parking lot in among the houses. There were no streets, just paths and dirt, no lawns and gardens, just sagebrush and dirt. Quite a few people were gathering or wandering around the open place, looking dressed up, wearing colorful shirts, print dresses, strings of beads, earrings. "Hey there, Chipmunk, Whitefoot!" they greeted the women.

A man in new jeans, with a bright blue velveteen vest over a clean, faded blue workshirt, came forward to meet them, very handsome, tense, and important. "All right, Gal!" he said in a harsh, loud voice, which startled among all these soft-speaking people. "We're going to get that eye fixed right up tonight! You just sit down here and don't worry about a thing." He took her wrist, gently despite his bossy, brassy manner, and led her to a woven mat that lay on the dirt near the middle of the open place. There, feeling very foolish, she had to sit down, and was told to stay still. She soon got over feeling that everybody was looking at her, since nobody paid her more attention than a checking glance or, from Chipmunk or Whitefoot and their families, a reassuring wink. Every now and then Jay rushed over to her and said something like, "Going to be as good as new!" and went off again to organize people, waving his long blue arms and shouting.

Coming up the hill to the open place, a lean, loose, tawny figure—and the child started to jump up, remembered she was to sit still, and sat still, calling out softly, "Coyote! Coyote!"

Coyote came lounging by. She grinned. She stood looking down at the child. "Don't let that Bluejay fuck you up, Gal," she said, and lounged on.

The child's gaze followed her, yearning.

People were sitting down now over on one side of the open place, making an uneven half-circle that kept getting added to at the ends until there was nearly a circle of people sitting on the dirt around the child, ten or fifteen paces from her. All the people wore the kind of clothes the child was used to, jeans and jeans-jackets, shirts, vests, cotton dresses, but they were all barefoot; and she thought they were more beautiful than the people she knew, each in a different way, as if each one had invented beauty. Yet some of them were also very strange: thin black shining people with whispery voices, a long-legged woman with eyes like jewels. The big man called Young Owl was there, sleepy-looking and dignified, like Judge McCown who owned a sixty-thousand acre ranch; and beside him was a woman the child thought might be his sister, for like him she had a hook nose and big, strong hands; but she was lean and dark, and there was a crazy look in her fierce eyes. Yellow eyes, but round, not long and slanted like Coyote's. There was Coyote sitting yawning, scratching her armpit, bored. Now somebody was entering the circle: a man, wearing only a kind of kilt and a cloak painted or beaded with diamond shapes, dancing to the rhythm of the rattle he carried and shook with a buzzing fast beat. His limbs and body were thick yet supple, his movements smooth and pouring. The child kept her gaze on him as he danced past her, around her, past again. The rattle in his hand shook almost too fast to see, in the other hand was something thin and sharp. People were singing around the circle now, a few notes repeated in time to the rattle, soft and tuneless. It was exciting and boring, strange and familiar. The Rattler wove his dancing closer and closer to her, darting at her. The first time she flinched away, frightened by the lunging movement and by his flat, cold face with narrow eyes, but after that she sat still, knowing her part. The dancing went on, the singing went on, till they carried her past boredom into a floating that could go on forever.

Jay had come strutting into the circle, and was standing beside her. He couldn't sing, but he called out, "Hey! Hey! Hey! Hey!" in his big, harsh voice, and everybody answered from all round, and the echo came down from the rimrock on the second beat. Jay was holding up a stick with a ball on it in one hand, and something like a marble in the other. The stick was a pipe: he got smoke into his mouth from it and blew it in four directions and up and down and then over the marble, a puff each time. Then the rattle stopped suddenly, and everything was silent for several breaths. Jay squatted down and looked intently into the child's face, his head cocked to one side. He reached forward, muttering something in time to the rattle and the singing that had started up again louder than before; he touched the child's right eye in the black center of the pain. She flinched and endured. His touch was not gentle. She saw the marble, a dull yellow ball like beeswax, in his hand; then she shut her seeing eye and set her teeth.

"There!" Jay shouted. "Open up. Come on! Let's see!"

Her jaw clenched like a vise, she opened both eyes. The lid of the right one stuck and dragged with such a searing white pain that she nearly threw up as she sat there in the middle of everybody watching.

"Hey, can you see? How's it work? It looks great!" Jay was shaking her arm, railing at her. "How's it feel? Is it working?"

What she saw was confused, hazy, yellowish. She began to discover, as everybody came crowding around peering at her, smiling, stroking and patting her arms and shoulders, that if she shut the hurting eye and looked with the other, everything was clear and flat; if she used them both, things were blurry and yellowish, but deep.

There, right close, was Coyote's long nose and narrow

eyes and grin. "What is it, Jay?" she was asking, peering at the new eye. "One of mine you stole that time?"

"It's pine pitch," Jay shouted furiously. "You think I'd use some stupid secondhand coyote eye? I'm a doctor!"

"Ooooh, ooooh, a doctor," Coyote said. "Boy, that is one ugly eye. Why didn't you ask Rabbit for a rabbit-dropping? That eye looks like shit." She put her lean face yet closer, till the child thought she was going to kiss her; instead, the thin, firm tongue once more licked accurate across the pain, cooling, clearing. When the child opened both eyes again the world looked pretty good.

"It works fine," she said.

"Hey!" Jay yelled. "She says it works fine! It works fine, she says so! I told you! What'd I tell you?" He went off waving his arms and yelling. Coyote had disappeared. Everybody was wandering off.

The child stood up, stiff from long sitting. It was nearly dark; only the long west held a great depth of pale radiance. Eastward the plains ran down into night.

Lights were on in some of the shanties. Off at the edge of town somebody was playing a creaky fiddle, a lonesome chirping tune.

A person came beside her and spoke quietly: "Where will you stay?"

"I don't know," the child said. She was feeling extremely hungry. "Can I stay with Coyote?"

"She isn't home much," the soft-voiced woman said. "You were staying with Chipmunk, weren't you? Or there's Rabbit, or Jackrabbit, they have families..."

"Do you have a family?" the girl asked, looking at the delicate, soft-eyed woman.

"Two fawns," the woman answered, smiling. "But I just came into town for the dance."

"I'd really like to stay with Coyote," the child said after a little pause, timid, but obstinate.

"OK, that's fine. Her house is over here." Doe walked along beside the child to a ramshackle cabin on the high edge of town. No light shone from inside. A lot of junk was scattered around the front. There was no step up to the half-open door. Over the door a battered pine board, nailed up crooked, said BIDE-A-WEE.

"Hey, Coyote? Visitors," Doe said. Nothing happened.

Doe pushed the door farther open and peered in. "She's out hunting, I guess. I better be getting back to the fawns. You going to be OK? Anybody else here will give you something to eat—you know . . . OK?"

"Yeah. I'm fine. Thank you," the child said.

She watched Doe walk away through the clear twilight, a severely elegant walk, small steps, like a woman in high heels, quick, precise, very light.

Inside Bide-A-Wee it was too dark to see anything and so cluttered that she fell over something at every step. She could not figure out where or how to light a fire. There was something that felt like a bed, but when she lay down on it, it felt more like a dirty-clothes pile, and smelt like one. Things bit her legs, arms, neck, and back. She was terribly hungry. By smell she found her way to what had to be a dead fish hanging from the ceiling in one corner. By feel she broke off a greasy flake and tasted it. It was smoked dried salmon. She ate one succulent piece after another until she was satisfied, and licked her fingers clean. Near the open door starlight shone on water in a pot of some kind; the child smelled it cautiously, tasted it cautiously, and drank just enough to quench her thirst, for it tasted of mud and was warm and stale. Then she went back to the bed of dirty clothes and fleas, and lay down. She could have gone to Chipmunk's house, or other friendly households; she thought of that as she lay forlorn in Coyote's dirty bed. But she did not go. She slapped at fleas until she fell asleep.

Along in the deep night somebody said, "Move over, pup," and was warm beside her.

. . .

Breakfast, eaten sitting in the sun in the doorway, was dried-salmon-powder mush. Coyote hunted, mornings and evenings, but what they ate was not fresh game but salmon, and dried stuff, and any berries in season. The child did not ask about this. It made sense to her. She was going to ask Coyote why she slept at night and waked in the day like humans, instead of the other way round like coyotes, but when she framed the question in her mind she saw at once that night is when you sleep and day when you're awake; that made sense too. But one question she did ask, one hot day when they were lying around slapping fleas.

"I don't understand why you all look like people," she said.

"We are people."

"I mean, people like me, humans."

"Resemblance is in the eye," Coyote said. "How is that lousy eye, by the way?"

"It's fine. But—like you wear clothes—and live in houses —with fires and stuff—"

"That's what you think ... If that loudmouth Jay hadn't horned in, I could have done a really good job."

The child was quite used to Coyote's disinclination to stick to any one subject, and to her boasting. Coyote was like a lot of kids she knew, in some respects. Not in others.

"You mean what I'm seeing isn't true? Isn't real—like on TV, or something?"

"No," Coyote said. "Hey, that's a tick on your collar." She reached over, flicked the tick off, picked it up on one finger, bit it, and spat out the bits.

"Yecch!" the child said. "So?"

"So, to me you're basically greyish yellow and run on four legs. To that lot—" she waved disdainfully at the warren of little houses next down the hill—"you hop around twitching your nose all the time. To Hawk, you're an egg, or maybe getting pinfeathers. See? It just depends on how you look at things. There are only two kinds of people."

"Humans and animals?"

"No. The kind of people who say, 'There are two kinds of people' and the kind of people who don't." Coyote cracked up, pounding her thigh and yelling with delight at her joke. The child didn't get it, and waited.

"OK," Coyote said. "There's the first people, and then the others. That's the two kinds."

"The first people are—?"

"Us, the animals ... and things. All the old ones. You know. And you pups, kids, fledglings. All first people."

"And the—others?"

"Them," Coyote said. "You know. The others. The new people. The ones who came." Her fine, hard face had gone serious, rather formidable. She glanced directly, as she seldom did, at the child, a brief gold sharpness. "We were here," she said. "We were always here. We are always here. Where we are is here. But it's their country now. They're running it ... Shit, even I did better!"

The child pondered and offered a word she had used to hear a good deal: "They're illegal immigrants."

"Illegal!" Coyote said, mocking, sneering. "Illegal is a sick bird. What the fuck's illegal mean? You want a code of justice from a coyote? Grow up, kid!"

"I don't want to."

"You don't want to grow up?"

"I'll be the other kind if I do."

"Yeah. So," Coyote said, and shrugged. "That's life." She got up and went around the house, and the child heard her pissing in the back yard.

A lot of things were hard to take about Coyote as a mother. When her boyfriends came to visit, the child learned to go stay with Chipmunk or the Rabbits for the night, because Coyote and her friend wouldn't even wait to get on the bed but would start doing that right on the floor or even out in the yard. A couple of times Coyote came back late from hunting with a friend, and the child had to lie up against the wall in the same bed and hear and feel them doing that right next to her. It was something like fighting and something like dancing, with a beat to it, and she didn't mind too much except that it made it hard to stay asleep.

Once she woke up and one of Coyote's friends was stroking her stomach in a creepy way. She didn't know what to do, but Coyote woke up and realized what he was doing, bit him hard, and kicked him out of bed. He spent the night on the floor, and apologized next morning—"Aw, hell, Ki, I forgot the kid was there, I thought it was you—"

Coyote, unappeased, yelled, "You think I don't got any standards? You think I'd let some coyote rape a kid in my bed?" She kicked him out of the house, and grumbled about him all day. But a while later he spent the night again, and he and Coyote did that three or four times.

Another thing that was embarrassing was the way Coyote peed anywhere, taking her pants down in public. But most people here didn't seem to care. The thing that worried the child most, maybe, was when Coyote did number two anywhere and then turned around and talked to it. That seemed so awful. As if Coyote was—the way she often seemed, but really wasn't—crazy.

The child gathered up all the old dry turds from around the house one day while Coyote was having a nap, and buried them in a sandy place near where she and Bobcat and some of the other people generally went and did and buried their number twos.

Coyote woke up, came lounging out of Bide-A-Wee, rubbing her hands through her thick, fair, greyish hair and yawning, looked all around once with those narrow eyes, and said, "Hey! Where are they?" Then she shouted, "Where are you? Where are you?"

And a faint, muffled chorus came from over in the sandy draw, "Mommy! Mommy! We're here!"

Coyote trotted over, squatted down, raked out every turd, and talked with them for a long time. When she came back she said nothing, but the child, redfaced and heart pounding, said, "I'm sorry I did that."

"It's just easier when they're all around close by," Coyote said, washing her hands (despite the filth of her house, she kept herself quite clean, in her own fashion.)

"I kept stepping on them," the child said, trying to justify her deed.

"Poor little shits," said Coyote, practicing dance-steps.

"Coyote," the child said timidly. "Did you ever have any children? I mean real pups?"

"Did I? Did I have children? Litters! That one that tried feeling you up, you know? that was my son. Pick of the litter . . . Listen, Gal. Have daughters. When you have anything, have daughters. At least they clear out."

iii

The child thought of herself as Gal, but also sometimes as Myra. So far as she knew, she was the only person in town who had two names. She had to think about that, and about what Coyote had said about the two kinds of people; she had to think about where she belonged. Some persons in town made it clear that as far as they were concerned she didn't and never would belong there. Hawk's furious stare burned through her; the Skunk children made audible remarks about what she smelled like. And though White-foot and Chipmunk and their families were kind, it was the generosity of big families, where one more or less simply doesn't count. If one of them, or Cottontail, or Jackrabbit, had come upon her in the desert lying lost and half-blind, would they have stayed with her, like Coyote? That was Coyote's craziness, what they called her craziness. She wasn't afraid. She went between the two kinds of people, she crossed over. Buck and Doe and their beautiful children weren't really afraid, because they lived so constantly in danger. The Rattler wasn't afraid, because he was so dangerous. And yet maybe he was afraid of her, for he never spoke, and never came close to her. None of them treated her the way Coyote did. Even among the children, her only constant playmate was one younger than herself, a preposterous and fearless little boy called Horned Toad Child. They dug and built together, out among the sagebrush, and played at hunting and gathering and keeping house and holding dances, all the great games. A pale, squatty child with fringed eyebrows, he was a self-contained but loyal friend; and he knew a good deal for his age.

"There isn't anybody else like me here," she said, as they sat by the pool in the morning sunlight.

"There isn't anybody much like me anywhere," said Horned Toad Child.

"Well, you know what I mean."

"Yeah . . . There used to be people like you around, I guess."

"What were they called?"

"Oh—people. Like everybody . . ."

"But where do my people live? They have towns. I used to live in one. I don't know where they are, is all. I ought to find out. I don't know where my mother is now, but my daddy's in Canyonville. I was going there when."

"Ask Horse," said Horned Toad Child, sagaciously. He had moved away from the water, which he did not like and never drank, and was plaiting rushes.

"I don't know Horse."

"He hangs around the butte down there a lot of the time. He's waiting till his uncle gets old and he can kick him out and be the big honcho. The old man and the women don't want him around till then. Horses are weird. Anyway, he's the one to ask. He gets around a lot. And his people came here with the new people, that's what they say, anyhow."

Illegal immigrants, the girl thought. She took Horned Toad's advice, and one long day when Coyote was gone on one of her unannounced and unexplained trips, she took a pouchful of dried salmon and salmonberries and went off alone to the flat-topped butte miles away in the southwest.

There was a beautiful spring at the foot of the butte, and a trail to it with a lot of footprints on it. She waited there under willows by the clear pool, and after a while Horse came running, splendid, with copper-red skin and long, strong legs, deep chest, dark eyes, his black hair whipping his back as he ran. He stopped, not at all winded, and gave a snort as he looked at her. "Who are you?"

Nobody in town asked that—ever. She saw it was true: Horse had come here with her people, people who had to ask each other who they were.

"I live with Coyote," she said, cautiously.

"Oh, sure, I heard about you," Horse said. He knelt to drink from the pool, long deep drafts, his hands plunged in the cool water. When he had drunk he wiped his mouth, sat back on his heels, and announced, "I'm going to be king."

"King of the Horses?"

"Right! Pretty soon now. I could lick the old man already, but I can wait. Let him have his day," said Horse, vainglorious, magnanimous. The child gazed at him, in love already, forever.

"I can comb your hair, if you like," she said.

"Great!" said Horse, and sat still while she stood behind him, tugging her pocket comb through his coarse, black, shining, yard-long hair. It took a long time to get it smooth.

She tied it in a massive ponytail with willowbark when she was done. Horse bent over the pool to admire himself. "That's great," he said. "That's really beautiful!"

"Do you ever go...where the other people are?" she asked in a low voice.

He did not reply for long enough that she thought he wasn't going to; then he said, "You mean the metal places, the glass places? The holes? I go around them. There are all the walls now. There didn't used to be so many. Grandmother said there didn't used to be any walls. Do you know Grandmother?" he asked naively, looking at her with his great, dark eyes.

"Your grandmother?"

"Well, yes—Grandmother—You know. Who makes the web. Well, anyhow. I know there's some of my people, horses, there. I've seen them across the walls. They act really crazy. You know, we brought the new people here. They couldn't have got here without us, they only have two legs, and they have those metal shells. I can tell you that whole story. The King has to know the stories."

"I like stories a lot."

"It takes three nights to tell it. What do you want to know about them?"

"I was thinking that maybe I ought to go there. Where they are."

"It's dangerous. Really dangerous. You can't go through —they'd catch you."

"I'd just like to know the way."

"I know the way," Horse said, sounding for the first time entirely adult and reliable; she knew he did know the way. "It's a long run for a colt." He looked at her again. "I've got a cousin with different-color eyes," he said, looking from her right to her left eye. "One brown and one blue. But she's an Appaloosa."

"Bluejay made the yellow one," the child explained. "I

lost my own one. In the . . . when . . . You don't think I could get to those places?"

"Why do you want to?"

"I sort of feel like I have to."

Horse nodded. He got up. She stood still.

"I could take you, I guess," he said.

"Would you? When?"

"Oh, now, I guess. Once I'm King I won't be able to leave, you know. Have to protect the women. And I sure wouldn't let my people get anywhere near those places!" A shudder ran right down his magnificent body, yet he said, with a toss of his head, "They couldn't catch me, of course, but the others can't run like I do . . ."

"How long would it take us?"

Horse thought a while. "Well, the nearest place like that is over by the red rocks. If we left now we'd be back here around tomorrow noon. It's just a little hole."

She did not know what he meant by "a hole," but did not ask.

"You want to go?" Horse said, flipping back his ponytail.

"OK," the girl said, feeling the ground go out from under her.

"Can you run?"

She shook her head. "I walked here, though."

Horse laughed, a large, cheerful laugh. "Come on," he said, and knelt and held his hands backturned like stirrups for her to mount to his shoulders. "What do they call you?" he teased, rising easily, setting right off at a jogtrot. "Gnat? Fly? Flea?"

"Tick, because I stick!" the child cried, gripping the willowbark tie of the black mane, laughing with delight at being suddenly eight feet tall and traveling across the desert without even trying, like the tumbleweed, as fast as the wind.

. . .

Moon, a night past full, rose to light the plains for them. Horse jogged easily on and on. Somewhere deep in the night they stopped at a Pygmy Owl camp, ate a little, and rested. Most of the owls were out hunting, but an old lady entertained them at her campfire, telling them tales about the ghost of a cricket, about the great invisible people, tales that the child heard interwoven with her own dreams as she dozed and half-woke and dozed again. Then Horse put her up on his shoulders and on they went at a tireless slow lope. Moon went down behind them, and before them the sky paled into rose and gold. The soft nightwind was gone; the air was sharp, cold, still. On it, in it, there was a faint, sour smell of burning. The child felt Horse's gait change, grow tighter, uneasy.

"Hey, Prince!"

A small, slightly scolding voice: the child knew it, and placed it as soon as she saw the person sitting by a juniper tree, neatly dressed, wearing an old black cap.

"Hey, Chickadee!" Horse said, coming round and stopping. The child had observed, back in Coyote's town, that everybody treated Chickadee with respect. She didn't see why. Chickadee seemed an ordinary person, busy and talkative like most of the small birds, nothing like so endearing as Quail or so impressive as Hawk or Great Owl.

"You're going on that way?" Chickadee asked Horse.

"The little one wants to see if her people are living there," Horse said, surprising the child. Was that what she wanted?

Chickadee looked disapproving, as she often did. She whistled a few notes thoughtfully, another of her habits, and then got up. "I'll come along."

"That's great," Horse said, thankfully.

"I'll scout," Chickadee said, and off she went, surprisingly fast, ahead of them, while Horse took up his steady long lope.

The sour smell was stronger in the air.

Chickadee halted, way ahead of them on a slight rise, and stood still. Horse dropped to a walk, and then stopped. "There," he said in a low voice.

The child stared. In the strange light and slight mist before sunrise she could not see clearly, and when she strained and peered she felt as if her left eye were not seeing at all. "What is it?" she whispered.

"One of the holes. Across the wall—see?"

It did seem there was a line, a straight, jerky line drawn across the sagebrush plain, and on the far side of it—nothing? Was it mist? Something moved there—"It's cattle!" she said. Horse stood silent, uneasy. Chickadee was coming back towards them.

"It's a ranch," the child said. "That's a fence. There's a lot of Herefords." The words tasted like iron, like salt in her mouth. The things she named wavered in her sight and faded, leaving nothing—a hole in the world, a burned place like a cigarette burn. "Go closer!" she urged Horse. "I want to see."

And as if he owed her obedience, he went forward, tense but unquestioning.

Chickadee came up to them. "Nobody around," she said in her small, dry voice, "but there's one of those fast turtle things coming."

Horse nodded, but kept going forward.

Gripping his broad shoulders, the child stared into the blank, and as if Chickadee's words had focused her eyes, she saw again: the scattered whitefaces, a few of them looking up with bluish, rolling eyes—the fences—over the rise a chimneyed house-roof and a high barn—and then in the distance something moving fast, too fast, burning across the ground straight at them at terrible speed. "Run!" she yelled to Horse, "run away! Run!" As if released from bonds he wheeled and ran, flat out, in great reaching strides, away from sunrise, the fiery burning chariot, the smell of acid, iron, death. And Chickadee flew before them like a cinder on the air of dawn.

iv

"Horse?" Coyote said. "That prick? Catfood!"

Coyote had been there when the child got home to Bide-A-Wee, but she clearly hadn't been worrying about where Gal was, and maybe hadn't even noticed she was gone. She was in a vile mood, and took it all wrong when the child tried to tell her where she had been.

"If you're going to do damn fool things, next time do 'em with me, at least I'm an expert," she said, morose, and slouched out the door. The child saw her squatting down, poking an old, white turd with a stick, trying to get it to answer some question she kept asking it. The turd lay obstinately silent. Later in the day the child saw two coyote men, a young one and a mangy-looking older one, loitering around near the spring, looking over at Bide-A-Wee. She decided it would be a good night to spend somewhere else.

The thought of the crowded rooms of Chipmunk's house was not attractive. It was going to be a warm night again tonight, and moonlit. Maybe she would sleep outside. If she could feel sure some people wouldn't come around, like the Rattler...She was standing indecisive halfway through town when a dry voice said, "Hey, Gal."

"Hey, Chickadee."

The trim, black-capped woman was standing on her doorstep shaking out a rug. She kept her house neat, trim like herself. Having come back across the desert with her the child now knew, though she still could not have said, why Chickadee was a respected person.

"I thought maybe I'd sleep out tonight," the child said, tentative.

"Unhealthy," said Chickadee. "What are nests for?"

"Mom's kind of busy," the child said.

"Tsk!" went Chickadee, and snapped the rug with disapproving vigor. "What about your little friend? At least they're decent people."

"Horny-toad? His parents are so shy . . ."

"Well. Come in and have something to eat, anyhow," said Chickadee.

The child helped her cook dinner. She knew now why there were rocks in the mush-pot.

"Chickadee," she said, "I still don't understand, can I ask you? Mom said it depends who's seeing it, but still, I mean if I see you wearing clothes and everything like humans, then how come you cook this way, in baskets, you know, and there aren't any—any of the things like they have— there where we were with Horse this morning?"

"I don't know," Chickadee said. Her voice indoors was quite soft and pleasant. "I guess we do things the way they always were done. When your people and my people lived together, you know. And together with everything else here. The rocks, you know. The plants and everything." She looked at the basket of willowbark, fernroot, and pitch, at the blackened rocks that were heating in the fire. "You see how it all goes together . . .?

"But you have fire—That's different—"

"Ah!" said Chickadee, impatient, "you people! Do you think you invented the sun?"

She took up the wooden tongs, plopped the heated rocks into the water-filled basket with a terrific hiss and steam and loud bubblings. The child sprinkled in the pounded seeds, and stirred.

Chickadee brought out a basket of fine blackberries. They sat on the newly-shaken-out rug, and ate. The child's two-finger scoop technique with mush was now highly refined.

"Maybe I didn't cause the world," Chickadee said, "but I'm a better cook than Coyote."

The child nodded, stuffing.

"I don't know why I made Horse go there," she said, after she had stuffed. "I got just as scared as him when I saw it. But now I feel again like I have to go back there. But I want to stay here. With my, with Coyote. I don't understand."

"When we lived together it was all one place," Chickadee said in her slow, soft home-voice. "But now the others, the new people, they live apart. And their places are so heavy. They weigh down on our place, they press on it, draw it, suck it, eat it, eat holes in it, crowd it out... Maybe after a while longer there'll only be one place again, their place. And none of us here. I knew Bison, out over the mountains. I knew Antelope right here. I knew Grizzly and Greywolf, up west there. Gone. All gone. And the salmon you eat at Coyote's house, those are the dream salmon, those are the true food; but in the rivers, how many salmon now? The rivers that were red with them in spring? Who dances, now, when the First Salmon offers himself? Who dances by the river? Oh, you should ask Coyote about all this. She knows more than I do! But she forgets... She's hopeless, worse than Raven, she has to piss on every post, she's a terrible housekeeper..." Chickadee's voice had sharpened. She whistled a note or two, and said no more.

After a while the child asked very softly, "Who is Grandmother?"

"Grandmother," Chickadee said. She looked at the child, and ate several blackberries thoughtfully. She stroked the rug they sat on.

"If I built the fire on the rug, it would burn a hole in it," she said. "Right? So we build the fire on sand, on dirt... Things are woven together. So we call the weaver the Grandmother." She whistled four notes, looking up the smokehole. "After all," she added, "maybe all this place, the other places too, maybe they're all only one side of the weaving. I don't know. I can only look with one eye at a time, how can I tell how deep it goes?"

Lying that night rolled up in a blanket in Chickadee's back yard, the child heard the wind soughing and storming in the cottonwoods down in the draw, and then slept deeply, weary from the long night before. Just at sunrise she woke. The eastern mountains were a cloudy dark red as if the level light shone through them as through a hand held before the fire. In the tobacco patch—the only farming anybody in this town did was to raise a little wild tobacco—Lizard and Beetle were singing some kind of growing song or blessing song, soft and desultory, huh-huh-huh-huh, huh-huh-huh-huh, and as she lay warm-curled on the ground the song made her feel rooted in the ground, cradled on it and in it, so where her fingers ended and the dirt began she did not know, as if she were dead, but she was wholly alive, she was the earth's life. She got up dancing, left the blanket folded neatly on Chickadee's neat and already empty bed, and danced up the hill to Bide-A-Wee. At the half-open door she sang,

> "Danced with a gal with a hole in her stocking
> And her knees kept a knocking and her toes kept
>   a rocking,
> Danced with a gal with a hole in her stocking,
> Danced by the light of the moon!"

Coyote emerged, tousled and lurching, and eyed her narrowly. "Sheeeoot," she said. She sucked her teeth and then went to splash water all over her head from the gourd by the door. She shook her head and the water-drops flew. "Let's get out of here," she said. "I have had it. I don't know what got into me. If I'm pregnant again, at my age, oh, shit. Let's get out of town. I need a change of air."

In the foggy dark of the house, the child could see at least two coyote men sprawled snoring away on the bed and floor. Coyote walked over to the old white turd and kicked it. "Why didn't you stop me?" she shouted.

"I *told* you," the turd muttered sulkily.

"Dumb shit," Coyote said. "Come on, Gal. Let's go. Where to?" She didn't wait for an answer. "I know. Come on!"

And she set off through town at that lazy-looking rangy walk that was so hard to keep up with. But the child was full of pep, and came dancing, so that Coyote began dancing too, skipping and pirouetting and fooling around all the way down the long slope to the level plains. There she slanted their way off north-eastward. Horse Butte was at their backs, getting smaller in the distance.

Along near noon the child said, "I didn't bring anything to eat."

"Something will turn up," Coyote said, "sure to." And pretty soon she turned aside, going straight to a tiny grey shack hidden by a couple of half-dead junipers and a stand of rabbit-brush. The place smelled terrible. A sign on the door said: FOX. PRIVATE. NO TRESPASSING!—but Coyote pushed it open, and trotted right back out with half a small smoked salmon. "Nobody home but us chickens," she said, grinning sweetly.

"Isn't that stealing?" the child asked, worried.

"Yes," Coyote answered, trotting on.

They ate the fox-scented salmon by a dried-up creek, slept a while, and went on.

Before long the child smelled the sour burning smell, and stopped. It was as if a huge, heavy hand had begun pushing her chest, pushing her away, and yet at the same time as if she had stepped into a strong current that drew her forward, helpless.

"Hey, getting close!" Coyote said, and stopped to piss by a juniper stump.

"Close to what?"

"Their town. See?" She pointed to a pair of sage-spotted hills. Between them was an area of greyish blank.

"I don't want to go there."

"We won't go all the way in. No way! We'll just get a little closer and look. It's fun," Coyote said, putting her head on one side, coaxing. "They do all these weird things in the air."

The child hung back.

Coyote became business-like, responsible. "We're going to be very careful," she announced. "And look out for big dogs, OK? Little dogs I can handle. Make a good lunch. Big dogs, it goes the other way. Right? Let's go, then."

Seemingly as casual and lounging as ever, but with a tense alertness in the carriage of her head and the yellow glance of her eyes, Coyote led off again, not looking back; and the child followed.

All around them the pressures increased. It was if the air itself was pressing on them, as if time was going too fast, too hard, not flowing but pounding, pounding, pounding, faster and harder till it buzzed like Rattler's rattle. Hurry, you have to hurry! everything said, there isn't time! everything said. Things rushed past screaming and shuddering. Things turned, flashed, roared, stank, vanished. There was a boy—he came into focus all at once, but not on the ground: he was going along a couple of inches above the ground, moving very fast, bending his legs from side to side in a kind of frenzied swaying dance, and was gone. Twenty children sat in rows in the air all singing shrilly and then the walls closed over them. A basket no a pot no a can, a garbage can, full of salmon smelling wonderful no full of stinking deerhides and rotten cabbage stalks, keep out of it, Coyote! Where was she?

"Mom!" the child called. "Mother!"—standing a moment at the end of an ordinary small-town street near the gas station, and the next moment in a terror of blanknesses, invisible walls, terrible smells and pressures and the overwhelming rush of Time straight forward rolling her helpless as a twig in the race above a waterfall. She clung, held on trying not to fall—"Mother!"

Coyote was over by the big basket of salmon, approaching it, wary, but out in the open, in the full sunlight, in the full current. And a boy and a man borne by the same current were coming down the long, sage-spotted hill behind the gas station, each with a gun, red hats, hunters, it was killing season. "Hell, will you look at that damn coyote in broad daylight big as my wife's ass," the man said, and cocked aimed shot all as Myra screamed and ran against the enormous drowning torrent. Coyote fled past her yelling, "Get out of here!" She turned and was borne away.

Far out of sight of that place, in a little draw among low hills, they sat and breathed air in searing gasps until after a long time it came easy again.

"Mom, that was *stupid*," the child said furiously.

"Sure was," Coyote said. "But did you see all that food!"

"I'm not hungry," the child said sullenly. "Not till we get all the way away from here."

"But they're your folks," Coyote said. "All yours. Your kith and kin and cousins and kind. Bang! Pow! There's Coyote! Bang! There's my wife's ass! Pow! There's anything—BOOOOM! Blow it away, man! BOOOOOOM!"

"I want to go home," the child said.

"Not yet," said Coyote. "I got to take a shit." She did so, then turned to the fresh turd, leaning over it. "It says I have to stay," she reported, smiling.

"It didn't say anything! I was listening!"

"You know how to understand? You hear everything, Miss Big Ears? Hears all—Sees all with her crummy gummy eye—"

"You have pine-pitch eyes too! You told me so!"

"That's a story," Coyote snarled. "You don't even know a story when you hear one! Look, do what you like, it's a free country. I'm hanging around here tonight. I like the action." She sat down and began patting her hands on the dirt in a soft four-four rhythm and singing under her breath, one of the endless tuneless songs that kept time from running too fast, that wove the roots of trees and bushes and ferns and grass in the web that held the stream in the streambed and the rock in the rock's place and the earth together. And the child lay listening.

"I love you," she said.

Coyote went on singing.

Sun went down the last slope of the west and left a pale green clarity over the desert hills.

Coyote had stopped singing. She sniffed. "Hey," she said. "Dinner." She got up and moseyed along the little draw. "Yeah," she called back softly. "Come on!"

Stiffly, for the fear-crystals had not yet melted out of her joints, the child got up and went to Coyote. Off to one side along the hill was one of the lines, a fence. She didn't look at it. It was OK. They were outside it.

"Look at that!"

A smoked salmon, a whole chinook, lay on a little cedar-bark mat. "An offering! Well, I'll be darned!" Coyote was so impressed she didn't even swear. "I haven't seen one of these for years! I thought they'd forgotten!"

"Offering to who?"

"Me! Who else? Boy, *look* at that!"

The child looked dubiously at the salmon.

"It smells funny."

"How funny?"

"Like burned."

"It's smoked, stupid! Come on."

"I'm not hungry."

"OK. It's not your salmon anyhow. It's mine. My offering,

for me. Hey, you people! You people over there! Coyote thanks you! Keep it up like this and maybe I'll do some good things for you too!"

"Don't, don't yell, Mom! They're not that far away—"

"They're all my people," said Coyote with a great gesture, and then sat down cross-legged, broke off a big piece of salmon, and ate.

Evening Star burned like a deep, bright pool of water in the clear sky. Down over the twin hills was a dim suffusion of light, like a fog. The child looked away from it, back at the star.

"Oh," Coyote said. "Oh, shit."

"What's wrong?"

"That wasn't so smart, eating that," Coyote said, and then held herself and began to shiver, to scream, to choke—her eyes rolled up, her long arms and legs flew out jerking and dancing, foam spurted out between her clenched teeth. Her body arched tremendously backwards, and the child, trying to hold her, was thrown violently off by the spasms of her limbs. The child scrambled back and held the body as it spasmed again, twitched, quivered, went still.

By moonrise Coyote was cold. Till then there had been so much warmth under the tawny coat that the child kept thinking maybe she was alive, maybe if she just kept holding her, keeping her warm, she would recover, she would be all right. She held her close, not looking at the black lips drawn back from the teeth, the white balls of the eyes. But when the cold came through the fur as the presence of death, the child let the slight, stiff corpse lie down on the dirt.

She went nearby and dug a hole in the stony sand of the draw, a shallow pit. Coyote's people did not bury their dead, she knew that. But her people did. She carried the small corpse to the pit, laid it down, and covered it with her blue and white bandanna. It was not large enough; the four stiff paws stuck out. The child heaped the body over with sand and rocks and a scurf of sagebrush and tumbleweed held down with more rocks. She also went to where the salmon had lain on the cedar mat, and finding the carcass of a lamb heaped dirt and rocks over the poisoned thing. Then she stood up and walked away without looking back.

At the top of the hill she stood and looked across the draw toward the misty glow of the lights of the town lying in the pass between the twin hills.

"I hope you all die in pain," she said aloud. She turned away and walked down into the desert.

v

It was Chickadee who met her, on the second evening, north of Horse Butte.

"I didn't cry," the child said.

"None of us do," said Chickadee. "Come with me this way now. Come into Grandmother's house."

It was underground, but very large, dark and large, and the Grandmother was there at the center, at her loom. She was making a rug or blanket of the hills and the black rain and the white rain, weaving in the lightning. As they spoke she wove.

"Hello, Chickadee. Hello, New Person."

"Grandmother," Chickadee greeted her.

The child said, "I'm not one of them."

Grandmother's eyes were small and dim. She smiled and wove. The shuttle thrummed through the warp.

"Old Person, then," said Grandmother. "You'd better go back there now, Granddaughter. That's where you live."

"I lived with Coyote. She's dead. They killed her."

"Oh, don't worry about Coyote!" Grandmother said, with a little huff of laughter. "She gets killed all the time."

The child stood still. She saw the endless weaving.

"Then I—Could I go back home—to her house—?"

"I don't think it would work," Grandmother said. "Do you, Chickadee?"

Chickadee shook her head once, silent.

"It would be dark there now, and empty, and fleas . . . You got outside your people's time, into our place; but I think that Coyote was taking you back, see. Her way. If you go back now, you can still live with them. Isn't your father there?"

The child nodded.

"They've been looking for you."

"They have?"

"Oh, yes, ever since you fell out of the sky. The man was dead, but you weren't there—they kept looking."

"Serves him right. Serves them all right," the child said. She put her hands up over her face and began to cry terribly, without tears.

"Go on, little one, Granddaughter," Spider said. "Don't be afraid. You can live well there. I'll be there too, you know. In your dreams, in your ideas, in dark corners in the basement. Don't kill me, or I'll make it rain . . ."

"I'll come around," Chickadee said. "Make gardens for me."

The child held her breath and clenched her hands until her sobs stopped and let her speak.

"Will I ever see Coyote?"

"I don't know," the Grandmother replied.

The child accepted this. She said, after another silence, "Can I keep my eye?"

"Yes. You can keep your eye."

"Thank you, Grandmother," the child said. She turned away then and started up the night slope towards the next day. Ahead of her in the air of dawn for a long way a little bird flew, black-capped, light-winged.

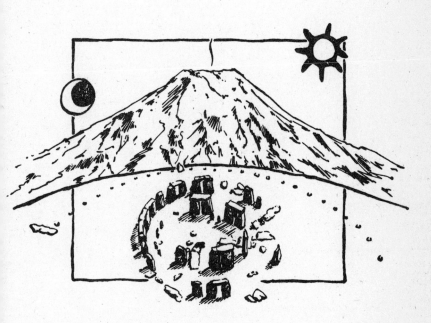

II

Three Rock Poems

The first thing about rocks is, they're old. What a geologist calls a "young" rock may be older than the species of the individual who picks it up to look at or throw at something or build with; even a genuinely new bit of pumice, fresh from the mouth of Mt. St. Helens, which spat it out into the Columbia River in 1981 to drift down and be picked up on a beach south of the rivermouth, is potentially (if one may say so) old—able to exist in its shapeless, chaotic thingness for time to come beyond human count of years. In the wonderful passage in T.H. White's Sword in the Stone *where young Arthur the Wart learns to understand what the rocks are saying, what he hears them whisper is, "Cohere. Cohere." Rocks are in time in a different way than living things are, even the ancient trees. So I was thinking when I came to the last line of the poem "Flints." But then, the other thing about rocks is that they* are place *(hence the next-to-last line). Rocks are what a place is made of to start with and after all. They are under everything else in the world, dirt, water, street, house, air, launching pad. The stone is at the center.*

The man and woman who survived the Greek Flood were told, "Cast your mother's bones behind you and don't look back." When they had figured out what their mother's bones were, they did so; and the rocks softened, and took form, and became flesh: our flesh. And this is indeed what happened, between the Pre-Cambrian Era and this week: the matter of Earth, rock, softened, took form, opened eyes, stood up, stooped down to pick up a rock in soft, warm, momentary fingers . . .

The Basalt

This rock land poured like milk.
Molten it flowed like honey.
Volcanoes told it,
their mouths told all the words of the story,
continuous, tremendous, coherent,
brimming over and flowing as easy
as milk and as certain as darkness.
You can pick up a word and hold it,
opaque,
untranslated.

(1982)

Flints

Color of sun on stone,
what color, grey or gold?
In winter Oregon
on Wiltshire flints in the window
the same sun. The same stones:
the standing woman,
the blind head,
the leaner, the turner, the stranger.
Bones of England, single stones
that mean the world,
that mean the world is old.

(1986)

Mount St. Helens /
Omphalos

O mountain there is no other
where you stand the center
is
    Seven stones in a circle
Robert Spott the shaman
set them
the child watched him
    There stands the Henge
a child plays with toy cars
on the Altar Stone
    There stands the mountain
alone and there is no other
center nor circle's edge
    O stone among the stars
the children on the moon
saw you
    and came home
Earth, hearth, hill, altar,
heart's home, the stone
is at the center

(1972)

III

"The Wife's Story" and "Mazes"

"Mazes" is a quite old story, and "The Wife's Story" a more recent one; what they have in common, it seems to me, is that they are both betrayals. They are simple but drastic reversals of the conventional, the expected. So strong is the sway of the expected that I have learned to explain before I read them to an audience that "The Wife's Story" is not about werewolves, and that "Mazes" is not about rats. Perhaps what confuses people in "Mazes" is that the character called 'the alien' is from what we call 'the earth,' and the other one isn't. The source of the resistance to the reversal in "The Wife's Story" may lie somewhat deeper.

Mazes

I have tried hard to use my wits and keep up my courage, but I know now that I will not be able to withstand the torture any longer. My perceptions of time are confused, but I think it has been several days since I realized I could no longer keep my emotions under aesthetic control, and now the physical breakdown is also nearly complete. I cannot accomplish any of the greater motions. I cannot speak. Breathing, in this heavy foreign air, grows more difficult. When the paralysis reaches my chest I shall die: probably tonight.

The alien's cruelty is refined, yet irrational. If it intended all along to starve me, why not simply withhold food? But instead of that it gave me plenty of food, mountains of food, all the greenbud leaves I could possibly want. Only they were not fresh. They had been picked; they were dead; the element that makes them digestible to us was gone, and one might as well eat gravel. Yet there they were, with all the scent and shape of greenbud, irresistible to my craving appetite. Not at first, of course. I told myself, I am not a child, to eat picked leaves! But the belly gets the better of the mind. After a while it seemed better to be chewing something, anything, that might still the pain and craving in the gut. So I ate, and ate, and starved. It is a relief, now, to be so weak I cannot eat.

The same elaborately perverse cruelty marks all its behavior. And the worst thing of all is just the one I welcomed with such relief and delight at first: the maze. I was badly disoriented at first, after the trapping, being handled by a giant, being dropped into a prison; and this place around the prison is disorienting, spatially disquieting, the strange, smooth, curved wall-ceiling is of an alien substance and its lines are meaningless to me. So when I was taken up and put down, amidst all this strangeness, in a maze, a recognizable, even familiar maze, it was a moment of strength and hope after great distress. It seemed pretty clear that I had been put in the maze as a kind of test or investigation, that a first approach toward communication was being attempted. I tried to cooperate in every way. But it was not possible to believe for very long that the creature's purpose was to achieve communication.

It is intelligent, highly intelligent, that is clear from a thousand evidences. We are both intelligent creatures, we are both maze-builders: surely it would be quite easy to learn to talk together! If that were what the alien wanted. But it is not. I do not know what kind of mazes it builds for itself. The ones it made for me were instruments of torture.

The mazes were, as I said, of basically familiar types, though the walls were of that foreign material much colder and smoother than packed clay. The alien left a pile of picked leaves in one extremity of each maze, I do not know why; it may be a ritual or superstition. The first maze it put me in was babyishly short and simple. Nothing expressive or even interesting could be worked out from it. The second, however, was a kind of simple version of the Ungated Affirmation, quite adequate for the reassuring, outreaching statement I wanted to make. And the last, the long maze, with seven corridors and nineteen connections, lent itself surprisingly well to the Maluvian mode, and indeed to almost all the New Expressionist techniques. Adaptations had to be made to the alien spatial understanding, but a certain quality of creativity arose precisely from the adaptations. I worked hard at the problem of that maze, planning all night long, re-imagining the lines and spaces, the feints and pauses, the erratic, unfamiliar, and yet beautiful course of the True Run. Next day when I was placed in the long maze and the alien began to observe, I performed the Eighth Maluvian in its entirety.

It was not a polished performance. I was nervous, and the spatio-temporal parameters were only approximate. But the Eighth Maluvian survives the crudest performance in the poorest maze. The evolutions in the ninth encatenation, where the "cloud" theme recurs so strangely transposed into the ancient spiraling motif, are indestructibly beautiful. I have seen them performed by a very old person, so old and stiff-jointed that he could only suggest the movements, hint at them, a shadow-gesture, a dim reflection of the themes: and all who watched were inexpressibly moved. There is no nobler statement of our being. Performing, I myself was carried away by the power of the motions and forgot that I was a prisoner, forgot the alien eyes watching me; I transcended the errors of the maze and my own weakness, and danced the Eighth Maluvian as I have never danced it before.

When it was done, the alien picked me up and set me down in the first maze—the short one, the maze for little children who have not yet learned how to talk.

Was the humiliation deliberate? Now that it is all past, I see that there is no way to know. But it remains very hard to ascribe its behavior to ignorance.

After all, it is not blind. It has eyes, recognizable eyes. They are enough like our eyes that it must see somewhat as we do. It has a mouth, four legs, can move bipedally, has grasping hands, etc.; for all its gigantism and strange looks, it seems less fundamentally different from us, physically, than a fish. And yet, fish school and dance and, in their own stupid way, communicate! The alien has never once attempted to talk with me. It has been with me, watched me, touched me, handled me, for days: but all its motions have been purposeful, not communicative. It is evidently a solitary creature, totally self-absorbed.

This would go far to explain its cruelty.

I noticed early that from time to time it would move its curious horizontal mouth in a series of fairly delicate, repetitive gestures, a little like someone eating. At first I thought it was jeering at me; then I wondered if it was trying to urge me to eat the indigestible fodder; then I wondered if it could be communicating *labially*. It seemed a limited and unhandy language for one so well provided with hands, feet, limbs, flexible spine, and all; but that would be like the creature's perversity, I thought. I studied its lip-motions and tried hard to imitate them. It did not respond. It stared at me briefly and then went away.

In fact, the only indubitable *response* I ever got from it was on a pitifully low level of interpersonal aesthetics. It was tormenting me with knob-pushing, as it did once a day. I had endured this grotesque routine pretty patiently for the first several days. If I pushed one knob I got a nasty sensation in my feet, if I pushed a second I got a nasty pellet of dried-up food, if I pushed a third I got nothing whatever. Obviously, to demonstrate my intelligence I was to push the third knob. But it appeared that my intelligence irritated my captor, because it removed the neutral knob after the second day. I could not imagine what it was trying to establish or accomplish, except the fact that I was its prisoner and a great deal smaller than it. When I tried to leave the knobs, it forced me physically to return. I must sit there pushing knobs for it, receiving punishment from one and mockery from the other. The deliberate outrageousness of the situation, the insufferable heaviness and thickness of this air, the feeling of being forever watched yet never understood, all combined to drive me into a condition for which we have no description at all. The nearest thing I can suggest is the last interlude of the Ten Gate Dream, when all the feintways are closed and the dance narrows in and in until it bursts terribly into the vertical. I cannot say what I felt, but it was a little like that. If I got my feet stung once more, or got pelted once more with a lump of rotten food, I would go vertical forever... I took the knobs off the wall (they came off with a sharp tug, like flowerbuds), laid them in the middle of the floor, and defecated on them.

The alien took me up at once and returned to my prison. It had got the message, and had acted on it. But how unbelievably primitive the message had had to be! And the next day, it put me back in the knob room, and there were the knobs as good as new, and I was to choose alternate punishments for its amusement... Until then I had told myself that the creature was alien, therefore incomprehensible and uncomprehending, perhaps not intelligent in the same *manner* as we, and so on. But since then I have known that, though all that may remain true, it is also unmistakably and grossly cruel.

When it put me into the baby maze yesterday, I could not move. The power of speech was all but gone (I am dancing this, of course, in my mind; "the best maze is the mind," the old proverb goes) and I simply crouched there, silent. After a while it took me out again, gently enough. There is the ultimate perversity of its behavior: it has never once touched me cruelly.

It set me down in the prison, locked the gate, and filled up the trough with inedible food. Then it stood two-legged, looking at me for a while.

Its face is very mobile, but if it speaks with its face I cannot understand it, that is too foreign a language. And its body is always covered with bulky, binding mats, like an old widower who has taken the Vow of Silence. But I had become accustomed to its great size, and to the angular character of its limb-positions, which at first had seemed to be saying a steady stream of incoherent and mispronounced phrases, a horrible nonsense-dance like the motions of an imbecile, until I realized that they were strictly purposive movements. Now I saw something a little beyond that, in its position. There were no words, yet there was communication. I saw, as it stood watching me, a clear signification of angry sadness—as clear as the Sembrian Stance. There was the same lax immobility, the bentness, the assertion of defeat. Never a word came clear, and yet it told me that it was filled with resentment, pity, impatience, and frustration. It told me it was sick of torturing me, and wanted me to help it. I am sure I understood it. I tried to answer. I tried to say, "What is it you want of me? Only tell me what it is you want." But I was too weak to speak clearly, and it did not understand. It has never understood.

And now I have to die. No doubt it will come in to watch me die; but it will not understand the dance I dance in dying. (1971)

The Wife's Story

HE WAS A GOOD HUSBAND, a good father. I don't
understand it. I don't believe in it. I don't believe that it
happened. I saw it happen but it isn't true. It can't be. He
was always gentle. If you'd have seen him playing with the
children, anybody who saw him with the children would
have known that there wasn't any bad in him, not one
mean bone. When I first met him he was still living with
his mother over near Spring Lake, and I used to see them
together, the mother and the sons, and think that any
young fellow that was that nice with his family must be
one worth knowing. Then one time when I was walking in
the woods I met him by himself coming back from a
hunting trip. He hadn't got any game at all, not so much as
a field mouse, but he wasn't cast down about it. He was just
larking along enjoying the morning air. That's one of the
things I first loved about him. He didn't take things hard,
he didn't grouch and whine when things didn't go his way.
So we got to talking that day. And I guess things moved
right along after that, because pretty soon he was over here
pretty near all the time. And my sister said—see, my parents had moved out the year before and gone South, leaving us the place—my sister said, kind of teasing but
serious, "Well! If he's going to be here every day and half
the night, I guess there isn't room for me!" And she moved
out—just down the way. We've always been real close, her
and me. That's the sort of thing doesn't ever change. I
couldn't ever have got through this bad time without my
sis.

Well, so he came to live here. And all I can say is, it was
the happy year of my life. He was just purely good to me. A

hard worker and never lazy, and so big and fine-looking. Everybody looked up to him, you know, young as he was. Lodge Meeting nights, more and more often they had him to lead the singing. He had such a beautiful voice, and he'd lead off strong, and the others following and joining in, high voices and low. It brings the shivers on me now to think of it, hearing it, nights when I'd stayed home from meeting when the children was babies—the singing coming up through the trees there, and the moonlight, summer nights, the full moon shining. I'll never hear anything so beautiful. I'll never know a joy like that again.

It was the moon, that's what they say. It's the moon's fault, and the blood. It was in his father's blood. I never knew his father, and now I wonder what become of him. He was from up Whitewater way, and had no kin around here. I always thought he went back there, but now I don't know. There was some talk about him, tales, that come out after what happened to my husband. It's something runs in the blood, they say, and it may never come out, but if it does, it's the change of the moon that does it. Always it happens in the dark of the moon. When everybody's home asleep. Something comes over the one that's got the curse in his blood, they say, and he gets up because he can't sleep, and goes out into the glaring sun, and goes off all alone—drawn to find those like him. And it may be so, because my husband would do that. I'd half rouse and say, "Where you going to?" and he'd say, "Oh, hunting, be back this evening," and it wasn't like him, even his voice was different. But I'd be so sleepy, and not wanting to wake the kids, and he was so good and responsible, it was no call of mine to go asking "Why?" and "Where?" and all like that.

So it happened that way maybe three times or four. He'd come back late, and worn out, and pretty near cross for one so sweet-tempered—not wanting to talk about it. I figured everybody got to bust out now and then, and nagging never helped anything. But it did begin to worry me. No so much that he went, but that he come back so tired and strange. Even, he smelled strange. It made my hair stand up on end. I could not endure it and I said, "What is that—those smells on you? All over you!" And he said, "I don't know," real short, and made like he was sleeping. But he went down when he thought I wasn't noticing, and washed and washed himself. But those smells stayed in his hair, and in our bed, for days.

And then the awful thing. I don't find it easy to tell about this. I want to cry when I have to bring it to my mind. Our youngest, the little one, my baby, she turned from her father. Just overnight. He come in and she got scared-looking, stiff, with her eyes wide, and then she begun to cry and try to hide behind me. She didn't yet talk plain but she was saying over and over, "Make it go away! Make it go away!"

The look in his eyes, just for one moment, when he heard that. That's what I don't want ever to remember. That's what I can't forget. The look in his eyes looking at his own child.

I said to the child, "Shame on you, what's got into you?"—scolding, but keeping her right up close to me at the same time, because I was frightened too. Frightened to shaking.

He looked away then and said something like, "Guess she just waked up dreaming," and passed it off that way. Or tried to. And so did I. And I got real mad with my baby when she kept on acting crazy scared of her own dad. But she couldn't help it and I couldn't change it.

He kept away that whole day. Because he knew, I guess. It was just beginning dark of the moon.

It was hot and close inside, and dark, and we'd all been asleep some while, when something woke me up. He wasn't there beside me. I heard a little stir in the passage, when I listened. So I got up, because I could bear it no longer. I went out into the passage, and it was light there, hard sunlight coming in from the door. And I saw him standing just outside, in the tall grass by the entrance. His head was hanging. Presently he sat down, like he felt weary, and looked down at his feet. I held still, inside, and watched—I didn't know what for.

And I saw what he saw. I saw the changing. In his feet, it was, first. They got long, each foot got longer, stretching out, the toes stretching out and the foot getting long, and fleshy, and white. And no hair on them.

The hair begun to come away all over his body. It was like his hair fried away in the sunlight and was gone. He was white all over, then, like a worm's skin. And he turned his face. It was changing while I looked. It got flatter and flatter, the mouth flat and wide, and the teeth grinning flat and dull, and the nose just a knob of flesh with nostril holes, and the ears gone, and the eyes gone blue—blue, with white rims around the blue—staring at me out of that flat, soft, white face.

He stood up then on two legs.

I saw him, I had to see him, my own dear love, turned into the hateful one.

I couldn't move, but as I crouched there in the passage staring out into the day I was trembling and shaking with a growl that burst out into a crazy, awful howling. A grief howl and a terror howl and a calling howl. And the others heard it, even sleeping, and woke up.

It stared and peered, that thing my husband had turned into, and shoved its face up to the entrance of our house. I was still bound by mortal fear, but behind me the children had waked up, and the baby was whimpering. The mother anger come into me then, and I snarled and crept forward.

The man thing looked around. It had no gun, like the ones from the man places do. But it picked up a heavy fallen tree-branch in its long white foot, and shoved the end of that down into our house, at me. I snapped the end of it in my teeth and started to force my way out, because I knew the man would kill our children if it could. But my sister was already coming. I saw her running at the man with her head low and her mane high and her eyes yellow as the winter sun. It turned on her and raised up that branch to hit her. But I come out of the doorway, mad with the mother anger, and the others all were coming answering my call, the whole pack gathering, there in that blind glare and heat of the sun at noon.

The man looked round at us and yelled out loud, and brandished the branch it held. Then it broke and ran, heading for the cleared fields and plowlands, down the mountainside. It ran, on two legs, leaping and weaving, and we followed it.

I was last, because love still bound the anger and the fear in me. I was running when I saw them pull it down. My sister's teeth were in its throat. I got there and it was dead. The others were drawing back from the kill, because of the taste of the blood, and the smell. The younger ones were cowering and some crying, and my sister rubbed her mouth against her forelegs over and over to get rid of the taste. I went up close because I thought if the thing was dead the spell, the curse must be done, and my husband could come back—alive, or even dead, if I could only see him, my true love, in his true form, beautiful. But only the dead man lay there white and bloody. We drew back and back from it, and turned and ran, back up into the hills, back to the woods of the shadows and the twilight and the blessed dark.

(1979)

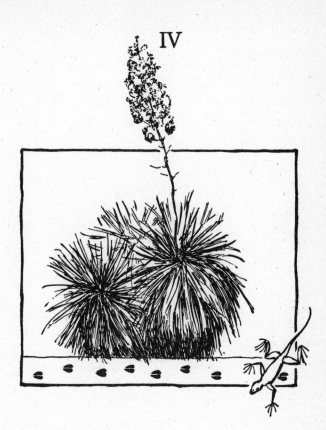

Five Vegetable Poems

The first four of these poems have to do with threat and survival, fragility and toughness, what lasts and what can't last. I think Westerners may sometimes perceive plants a bit differently from those who grew up where water can be taken for granted. In the West, one is often forced to see the plants as quite contingent. By now, however, anybody anywhere who can take trees for granted probably also believes that the so-called shortage of bison on the Great Plains is a liberal conspiracy.

The fifth poem, "The Crown of Laurel," is what Adrienne Rich has called a re-visioning. Myths are one of our most useful techniques of living, ways of telling the world, narrating reality, but in order to be useful they must (however archetypal and collectively human their structure) be retold; and the teller makes them over—and over. Many women and some men are now engaged in what almost seems a shared undertaking of re-telling, re-thinking the myths and tales we learned as children—fables, folktales, legends, hero-stories, god-stories. So John Gardner in his brilliant novel Grendel *(Beowulf as seen by the monster), and Anne Sexton's equally brilliant* Transformations *of folktales; and the work goes on, and this poem is part of it. Very often the re-visioning consists in a 'simple' change of point of view. It is possible that the very concept of point-of-view may be changing, may have to change, or to be changed, so that our reality can be narrated.*

Torrey Pines Reserve

(For Bob and Mary Elliott)

Ground dry as yellow bones.
A dust of sand, gold-mica-glittering.
Oh, dry! Grey ceanothus stems
twisted and tough; small flowers. A lizard place.
Rain rare and hard as an old woman's tears
runnelled these faces of the cliffs.
Sandstone is softer than the salty wind;
it crumbles, wrinkles, very old,
vulnerable. Circles in the rock
in hollows worn by ocean long ago.
These are eyes that were his pearls.
         One must walk
lightly; this is fragile.
Hold to the thread of way.
There's narrow place for us
in this high place between the still
desert and the stillness of the sea.
This gentle wilderness.

The Torrey pines
grow nowhere else on earth.

Listen:
you can hear the lizards
listening.

                                                (1973)

Lewis and Clark and After

Always in the solemn company
(save on the Desert Plains)
of those great beings (we did not
think much about it, trees
by our tribe being
seen with the one eye) we
walked across a forest continent.

Ohone! ohone! the deep groves,
the high woods of Ohio!
the fir-dark mountains, the silent lives,
the forests, the forests of Oregon!

(1985)

West Texas

Honor the lives of the terrible places:
greasewood, rabbitbrush, prickly pear,
yucca, swordfern, sagebrush,
the dingy wild-eyed sheep alert
and deer like shadows starting from the rock.
In gait and grace and stubborn strength
with delicate hoof or filament root,
stonebreakers, lifebringers.
Let there be rain for them.

(1980)

Xmas Over

The young fir in the back of the car
was silent, didn't admire the scenery,
took up residence without comment
in the high field near the old apple,
trading a two-foot pot for the Columbia Gorge.
When the wind came up, the branches
said Ssshhh to it, but the trunk and roots
were taciturn, and will be
a hundred years from now, perhaps.
Where the glass bubbles and colored lights
were, will be rain, and owls.
It won't hear carols sung again.
But then, it never listened.

(1982)

The Crown of Laurel

He liked to feel my fingers in his hair.
So he pulled them off me, wove a wreath of them,
and wears it at parades and contests,
my dying fingers with their kitchen smell
interlocked around his sunny curls.
Sometimes he rests on me a while.
Aside from that, he seems to have lost interest.

        It wasn't to preserve my 'virtue' that I ran!
What's a nymph like me
to do with something that belongs to men?
It's just I wasn't in the mood.
And he didn't care. It scared me.

The little goatleg boys can't even talk,
but still they wait till they can smell you feel
like humping with a goatleg in the woods,
rolling and scratching and laughing—they can laugh!—
poor little hairycocks, I miss them.
    When we were tired of that kind of thing
my sister nymphs and I would lie around,
and talk, and tease, and stroke, and chase, and stretch
out panting for another talk, and sleep
in the warm shadows side by side
under the leaves, and all was as we pleased.
    And then the mortal hunters of the deer,
the poachers, the deciduous shepherd-boys:
they'd stop and gape and stare with owly eyes,
not even hoping, even when I smiled . . .
New every spring, like daffodils, those boys.
But once for forty years I met one man
up on the sheep-cropped hills of Arcady.
I kissed his wrinkles, the ravines of time
I cannot enter, gazing in his eyes, whose dark
dimmed and deepened, seeing less always, till he died.
I came to his burial. Among the villagers
I walked behind his grey-haired wife.
She could have been Time's wife, my grandmother.
    And then there were my brothers of the streams,
O my river-lovers, with their silver tongues
so sweet to thirst! the cool, prolonged delight
of a river moving in me, of his flow and flow and flow!
    They send to my roots their kindness, even now,
and slowly I drink it from my mother's hands.

    So that was all I knew, until he came,
hard, bright, burning, dry, intent:
one will, instead of wantings meeting;
no center but himself, the Sun. A god

is like that, I suppose; he has to be.
But I never asked to meet a god,
let alone make love with one! Why did he think
I wanted to? And when I told him no,
what harm did he think it did him?
It can't be hard to find a girl agape
to love a big blond blue-eyed god.
He said so, said, "You're all alike."
He's seen us all; he knows. So, why me?

I guess that maybe it was time for me
to give up going naked, and get dressed.
And it took a god to make me do it.
Mother never could. So I put on
my brown, ribbed stockings, and my underwear
of silky cambium, and my green dress.
And I became my clothing, being what I wear.

I run no more; the winds dance me.
My sister, seamstress, sovereign comes
up from the dark below the roots
to mend my clothes in April. And I stand
in my green patience in the winter rains.

He honors me, he says, to wear
my fingers turning brown and brittle, clenched
in the bright hair of his head. He sings.

My silence crowns the song.

(1987)

V

"The Direction of the Road" and
"Vaster Than Empires And More Slow"

The relation of our species to plant life is one of total depen-
dence and total exploitation—the relation of an infant to its
mother. Without plants the earth would have remained bare
rock and water; without plant respiration we'd suffocate
promptly; without vegetable food (firsthand or, as in meat,
secondhand) we starve. There is no other food.

Deo, Demeter, the grain-mother, and her daughter/self Kore
the Maiden called Persephone, raped by the Godfather's
brother and buried to rise again, are myth-images of this
relationship, recognized by 'primitive' farmers as fundamental.
It is still fundamental, but can be completely ignored by a
modern city dweller whose actual experience of plants is
limited to florists' daisies and supermarket beans. The igno-
rance of the urban poor is blameless; the arrogant ignorance of
the urban educated, particularly those in government, is inex-
cusable. There is no excuse for deforestation, for acid rain, or
for the hunger of two-thirds of the children of the earth.

A very savvy genre, science fiction often acknowledges our
plant-dependence—filling a room in the spaceship with hydro-
ponic tanks, or 'terraforming' the new planet so the colonists
can raise grain—but with some notable exceptions (such as
the film Silent Running*), science fiction lacks much real inter-*
est in what's green. The absolute passivity of plants, along with
their absolute resistance to being replaced by an industrial-age
substitute (we can have iron horses, steel eagles, mechanical
brains, but robot wheat? Plastic spinach? If you believe in that

you must eat the little green hedge on your sushi plate) prob-ably makes them terminally uninteresting to the metal-minded and those to whom technology is not a way of living in the world, but a way of defeating it.

All the same, both the stories that follow are quite conven-tional science fiction. "The Direction of the Road" is yet another point-of-view shift, but with the attention focused on Relativity. "Vaster" is a story about boldly going where, etc. In it I was, in part, trying to talk about the obscure fear, called panic, which many of us feel when alone in wilderness. I have lost the trail on an Oregon mountain in logged-over second-growth forest, where my individual relation to the trees and undergrowth and soil and my relative position in their earth-and-ocean-wide realm, as an animal and as a human, were, you might say, brought home to me—but then, who's afraid of a goddam tree? We can wipe 'em all out—in a century by clearcutting in a generation by pollution, in the twinkling of an eye—

Direction of the Road

THEY DID NOT USE TO BE SO DEMANDING. They never hurried us into anything more than a gallop, and that was rare; most of the time it was just a jigjog foot-pace. And when one of them was on his own feet, it was a real pleasure to approach him. There was time to accomplish the entire act with style. There he'd be, work-ing his legs and arms the way they do, usually looking at the road, but often aside at the fields, or straight at me: and I'd approach him steadily but quite slowly, growing larger all the time, synchronizing the rate of approach and the rate of growth perfectly so that at the very moment that I'd finished enlarging from a tiny speck to my full size—sixty feet in those days—I was abreast of him and hung above him, loomed, towered, overshadowed him. Yet he would show no fear. Not even the children were afraid of me, though often they kept their eyes on me as I passed by and started to diminish.

Sometimes on a hot afternoon one of the adults would stop me right there at our meeting-place, and lie down with his back against mine for an hour or more. I didn't mind in the least. I have an excellent hill, good sun, good wind, good view; why should I mind standing still for an hour or an afternoon? It's only a relative stillness, after all. One need only look at the sun to realize how fast one is going; and then, one grows continually—especially in summer. In any case I was touched by the way they would entrust themselves to me, letting me lean against their little warm backs, and falling sound asleep there between my feet. I liked them. They have seldom lent us Grace as do the birds; but I really preferred them to squirrels.

In those days the horses used to work for them, and that too was enjoyable from my point of view. I particularly liked the canter, and got quite proficient at it. The surging and rhythmical motion accompanied shrinking and growing with a swaying and swooping, almost an illusion of flight. The gallop was less pleasant. It was jerky, pounding: one felt tossed about like a sapling in a gale. And then, the slow approach and growth, the moment of looming-over, and the slow retreat and diminishing, all that was lost during the gallop. One had to hurl oneself into it, cloppety-cloppety-cloppety! and the man usually too busy riding, and the horse too busy running, even to look up. But then, it didn't happen often. A horse is mortal, after all, and like all the loose creatures grows tired easily; so they didn't tire their horses unless there was urgent need. And they seemed not to have so many urgent needs, in those days.

It's been a long time since I had a gallop, and to tell the

truth I shouldn't mind having one. There was something invigorating about it, after all.

I remember the first motorcar I saw. Like most of us, I took it for a mortal, some kind of loose creature new to me. I was a bit startled, for after a hundred and thirty-two years I thought I knew all the local fauna. But a new thing is always interesting, in its trivial fashion, so I observed this one with attention. I approached it at a fair speed, about the rate of a canter, but in a new gait, suitable to the ungainly looks of the thing: an uncomfortable, bouncing, rolling, choking, jerking gait. Within two minutes, before I'd grown a foot tall, I knew it was no mortal creature, bound or loose or free. It was a making, like the carts the horses got hitched to. I thought it so very ill-made that I didn't expect it to return, once it gasped over the West Hill, and I heartily hoped it never would, for I disliked that jerking bounce.

But the thing took to a regular schedule, and so, perforce, did I. Daily at four I had to approach it, twitching and stuttering out of the West, and enlarge, loom-over, and diminish. Then at five back I had to come, poppeting along like a young jackrabbit for all my sixty feet, jigging and jouncing out of the East, until at last I got clear out of sight of the wretched little monster and could relax and loosen my limbs to the evening wind. There were always two of them inside the machine: a young male holding the wheel, and behind him an old female wrapped in rugs, glowering. If they ever said anything to each other I never heard it. In those days I overheard a good many conversations on the road, but not from that machine. The top of it was open, but it made so much noise that it overrode all voices, even the voice of the song-sparrow I had with me that year. The noise was almost as vile as the jouncing.

I am of a family of rigid principle and considerable self-respect. The Quercian motto is "Break but bend not," and I have always tried to uphold it. It was not only personal vanity, but family pride, you see, that was offended when I was forced to jounce and bounce in this fashion by a mere making.

The apple trees in the orchard at the foot of the hill did not seem to mind; but then, apples are tame. Their genes have been tampered with for centuries. Besides, they are herd creatures; no orchard tree can really form an opinion of its own.

I kept my own opinion to myself.

But I was very pleased when the motorcar ceased to plague us. All month went by without it, and all month I walked at men and trotted at horses most willingly, and even bobbed for a baby on its mother's arm, trying hard though unsuccessfully to keep in focus.

Next month, however—September it was, for the swallows had left a few days earlier—another of the machines appeared, a new one, suddenly dragging me and the road and our hill, the orchard, the fields, the farmhouse roof, all jigging and jouncing and racketing along from East to West; I went faster than a gallop, faster than I had ever gone before. I had scarcely time to loom, before I had to shrink right down again.

And the next day there came a different one.

Yearly then, weekly, daily, they became commoner. They became a major feature of the local Order of Things. The road was dug up and re-metalled, widened, finished off very smooth and nasty, like a slug's trail, with no ruts, pools, rocks, flowers, or shadows on it. There used to be a lot of little loose creatures on the road, grasshoppers, ants, toads, mice, foxes, and so on, most of them too small to move for, since they couldn't really see one. Now the wise creatures took to avoiding the road, and the unwise ones got squashed. I have seen all too many rabbits die in that fashion, right at my feet. I am thankful that I am an oak, and that though I may be wind-broken or uprooted, hewn or sawn, at least I cannot, under any circumstances, be squashed.

With the presence of many motorcars on the road at once, a new level of skill was required of me. As a mere seedling, as soon as I got my head above the weeds, I had learned the basic trick of going two directions at once. I learned it without thinking about it, under the simple pressure of circumstances on the first occasion that I saw a walker in the East and a horseman facing him in the West. I had to go two directions at once, and I did so. It's something we trees master without real effort, I suppose. I was nervous, but I succeeded in passing the rider and then shrinking away from him while at the same time I was still jigjogging towards the walker, and indeed passed him (no looming, back in those days!) only when I had got quite out of sight of the rider. I was proud of myself, being very young, that first time I did it; but it sounds more difficult than it really is. Since those days of course I had done it innumerable times, and thought nothing about it; I could do it in my sleep. But have you ever considered the feat accomplished, the skill involved, when a tree enlarges, simultaneously yet at slightly different rates and in slightly different manners, for each one of forty motorcar drivers facing two opposite directions, while at the same time diminishing for forty more who have got their backs to it, meanwhile remembering to loom over each single one at the right moment: and to do this minute after minute, hour after hour, from daybreak till nightfall or long after?

For my road had become a busy one; it worked all day long under almost continual traffic. It worked, and I worked. I did not jounce and bounce so much any more, but I had to run faster and faster: to grow enormously, to loom in a split second, to shrink to nothing, all in a hurry, without time to enjoy the action, and without rest: over and over and over.

Very few of the drivers bothered to look at me, not even a seeing glance. They seemed, indeed, not to see any more. They merely stared ahead. They seemed to believe that they were "going somewhere." Little mirrors were affixed to the front of their cars, at which they glanced to see where they had been; then they stared ahead again. I had thought that only beetles had this delusion of Progress. Beetles are always rushing about, and never looking up. I had always had a pretty low opinion of beetles. But at least they let me be.

I confess that sometimes, in the blessed nights of darkness with no moon to silver my crown and no stars occluding with my branches, when I could rest, I would think seriously of escaping my obligation to the general Order of Things: of *failing to move.* No, not seriously. Half-seriously. It was mere weariness. If even a silly, three-year-old, female pussy willow at the foot of the hill accepted her responsibility, and jounced and rolled and accelerated and grew and shrank for each motorcar on the road, was I, an oak, to shrink? Noblesse oblige, and I trust I have never dropped an acorn that did not know its duty.

For fifty or sixty years, then, I have upheld the Order of Things, and have done my share in supporting the human creatures' illusion that they are "going somewhere." And I am not unwilling to do so. But a truly terrible thing has occurred, which I wish to protest.

I do not mind going two directions at once; I do not mind growing and shrinking simultaneously; I do not mind moving, even at the disagreeable rate of sixty or seventy miles an hour. I am ready to go on doing all these things until I am felled or bulldozed. They're my job. But I do object, passionately, to being made eternal.

Eternity is none of my business. I am an oak, no more, no less. I have my duty, and I do it; I have my pleasures, and enjoy them, though they are fewer, since the birds are fewer, and the wind's foul. But, long-lived though I may be, impermanence is my right. Mortality is my privilege. And it has been taken from me.

It was taken from me on a rainy evening in March last year.

Fits and bursts of cars, as usual, filled the rapidly moving road in both directions. I was so busy hurtling along, enlarging, looming, diminishing, and the light was failing so fast, that I scarcely noticed what was happening until it happened. One of the drivers of one of the cars evidently felt that his need to "go somewhere" was exceptionally urgent, and so attempted to place his car in front of the car in front of it. This maneuver involves a temporary slanting of the Direction of the Road and a displacement onto the far side, the side which normally runs the other direction (and may I say that I admire the road very highly for its skill in executing such maneuvers, which must be difficult for an unliving creature, a mere making). Another car, however, happened to be quite near the urgent one, and facing it, as it changed sides; and the road could not do anything about it, being already overcrowded. To avoid impact with the facing car, the urgent car totally violated the Direction of the Road, swinging it round to North-South in its own terms, and so forcing me to leap directly at it. I had no choice. I had to move, and move fast—eighty-five miles an hour. I leapt: I loomed enormous, larger than I have ever loomed before. And then I hit the car.

I lost a considerable piece of bark, and, what's more serious, a fair bit of cambium layer; but as I was seventy-two feet tall and about nine feet in girth at the point of impact, no real harm was done. My branches trembled with the shock enough that a last-year's robin's nest was dislodged and fell; and I was so shaken that I groaned. It is the only time in my life that I have ever said anything out loud.

The motorcar screamed horribly. It was smashed by my blow, squashed, in fact. Its hinder parts were not much affected, but the forequarters knotted up and knurled together like an old root, and little bright bits of it flew all about and lay like brittle rain.

The driver had no time to say anything; I killed him instantly.

It is not this that I protest. I had to kill him. I had no choice, and therefore have no regret. What I protest, what I cannot endure, is this: as I leapt at him, he saw me. He looked up at last. He saw me as I have never been seen before, not even by a child, not even in the days when people looked at things. He saw me whole, and saw nothing else—then, or ever.

He saw me under the aspect of eternity. He confused me with eternity. And because he died in that moment of false vision, because it can never change, I am caught in it, eternally.

This is unendurable. I cannot uphold such an illusion. If the human creatures will not understand Relativity, very well; but they must understand Relatedness.

If it is necessary to the Order of Things, I will kill drivers of cars, though killing is not a duty usually required of oaks. But it is unjust to require me to play the part, not of the killer only, but of death. For I am not death. I am life: I am mortal.

If they wish to see death visibly in the world, that is their business, not mine. I will not act Eternity for them. Let them not turn to the trees for death. If that is what they want to see, let them look into one another's eyes and see it there.

(1974)

Vaster Than Empires
and More Slow

IT WAS ONLY DURING THE EARLIEST DECADES of the League that the Earth sent ships out on the enormously long voyages, beyond the pale, over the stars and far away. They were seeking for worlds which had not been seeded or settled by the Founders on Hain, truly alien worlds. All the Known Worlds went back to the Hainish Origin, and the Terrans, having been not only founded but salvaged by the Hainish, resented this. They wanted to get away from the family. They wanted to find somebody new. The Hainish, like tiresomely understanding parents, supported their explorations, and contributed ships and volunteers, as did several other worlds of the League.

All these volunteers to the Extreme Survey crews shared one peculiarity: they were of unsound mind.

What sane person, after all, would go out to collect information that would not be received for five or ten centuries? Cosmic mass interference had not yet been eliminated from the operation of the ansible, and so instantaneous communication was reliable only within a range of 120 lightyears. The explorers would be quite isolated. And of course they had no idea what they might come back to, if they came back. No normal human being who had experienced time-slippage of even a few decades between League worlds would volunteer for a round trip of centuries. The Surveyors were escapists, misfits. They were nuts.

Ten of them climbed aboard the ferry at Smeming Port, and made varyingly inept attempts to get to know one another during the three days the ferry took getting to their ship, *Gum.* Gum is a Cetian nickname, on the order of Baby or Pet. There were two Cetians on the team, two Hainishmen, one Beldene, and five Terrans; the Cetian-built ship was chartered by the Government of Earth. Her motley crew came aboard wriggling through the coupling tube one by one like apprehensive spermatozoa trying to fertilize the universe. The ferry left, and the navigator put *Gum* underway. She flitted for some hours on the edge of space a few hundred million miles from Smeming Port, and then abruptly vanished.

When, after 10 hours 29 minutes, or 256 years, *Gum* reappeared in normal space, she was supposed to be in the vicinity of Star KG-E-96651. Sure enough, there was the gold pinhead of the star. Somewhere within a four-hundred-million-kilometer sphere there was also a greenish planet, World 4470, as charted by a Cetian mapmaker. The ship now had to find the planet. This was not quite so easy as it might sound, given a four-hundred-million-kilometer haystack. And *Gum* couldn't bat about in planetary space at near lightspeed; if she did, she and Star KG-E-96651 and World 4470 might all end up going bang. She had to creep, using rocket propulsion, at a few hundred thousand miles an hour. The Mathematician/Navigator, Asnanifoil, knew pretty well where the planet ought to be, and thought they might raise it within ten E-days. Meanwhile the members of the Survey team got to know one another still better.

"I can't stand him," said Porlock, the Hard Scientist (chemistry, plus physics, astronomy, geology, etc.), and little blobs of spittle appeared on his mustache. "The man is insane. I can't imagine why he was passed as fit to join a Survey team, unless this is a deliberate experiment in non-compatibility, planned by the Authority, with us as guinea pigs."

"We generally use hamsters and Hainish gholes," said Mannon, the Soft Scientist (psychology, plus psychiatry, anthropology, ecology, etc.), politely; he was one of the Hainishmen. "Instead of guinea pigs. Well, you know, Mr. Osden is really a very rare case. In fact, he's the first fully cured case of Render's Syndrome—a variety of infantile autism which was thought to be incurable. The great Terran analyst Hammergeld reasoned that the cause of the autistic condition in this case is a supernormal empathic capacity, and developed an appropriate treatment. Mr. Osden is the first patient to undergo that treatment, in fact he lived with Dr. Hammergeld until he was eighteen. The therapy was completely successful."

"Successful?"

"Why, yes. He certainly is not autistic."

"No, he's intolerable!"

"Well, you see," said Mannon, gazing mildly at the saliva-flecks on Porlock's mustache, "the normal defensive-aggressive reaction between strangers meeting—let's say you and Mr. Osden just for example—is something you're scarcely aware of; habit, manners, inattention get you past it; you've learned to ignore it, to the point where you might even deny it exists. However, Mr. Osden, being an empath, feels it. Feels his feelings, and yours, and is hard put to say which is which. Let's say that there's a normal element of hostility towards any stranger in your emotional reaction to him when you meet him, plus a spontaneous dislike of his looks, or clothes, or handshake—it doesn't matter what. He feels that dislike. As his autistic defense has been unlearned, he resorts to an aggressive-defense mechanism, a response in kind to the aggression which you have unwittingly projected onto him." Mannon went on for quite a long time.

"Nothing gives a man the right to be such a bastard," Porlock said.

"He can't tune us out?" asked Harfex, the Biologist, another Hainishman.

"It's like hearing" said Olleroo, Assistant Hard Scientist, stopping over to paint her toenails with fluorescent lacquer. "No eyelids on your ears. No Off switch on empathy. He hears our feelings whether he wants to or not."

"Does he know what we're *thinking?*" asked Eskwana, the Engineer, looking round at the others in real dread.

"No," Porlock snapped. "Empathy's not telepathy! Nobody's got telepathy."

"Yet," said Mannon, with his little smile. "Just before I left Hain there was a most interesting report in from one of the recently discovered worlds, a hilfer named Rocannon reporting what appears to be a teachable telepathic technique existent among a mutated hominid race; I only saw a synopsis in the HILF Bulletin, but—" He went on. The others had learned that they could talk while Mannon went on talking; he did not seem to mind, nor even to miss much of what they said.

"Then why does he hate us?" Eskwana said.

"Nobody hates you, Ander honey," said Olleroo, daubing Eskwana's left thumbnail with fluorescent pink. The engineer flushed and smiled vaguely.

"He acts as if he hated us," said Haito, the Coordinator. She was a delicate-looking woman of pure Asian descent, with a surprising voice, husky, deep, and soft, like a young bullfrog. "Why, if he suffers from our hostility, does he increase it by constant attacks and insults? I can't say I think much of Dr. Hammergeld's cure, really, Mannon; autism might be preferable..."

She stopped. Osden had come into the main cabin.

He looked flayed. His skin was unnaturally white and thin, showing the channels of his blood like a faded road map in red and blue. His Adam's apple, the muscles that circled his mouth, the bones and ligaments of his wrists and hands, all stood out distinctly as if displayed for an anatomy lesson. His hair was pale rust, like long-dried blood. He had eyebrows and lashes, but they were visible only in certain lights; what one saw was the bones of the eye sockets, the veining of the lids, and the colorless eyes. They were not red eyes, for he was not really an albino, but they were not blue or grey; colors had canceled out in Osden's eyes, leaving a cold water-like clarity, infinitely penetrable. He never looked directly at one. His face lacked expression, like an anatomical drawing, or a skinned face.

"I agree," he said in a high, harsh tenor, "that even autistic withdrawal might be preferable to the smog of cheap secondhand emotions with which you people surround me. What are you sweating hate for now, Porlock? Can't stand the sight of me? Go practice some auto-eroticism the way you were doing last night, it improves your vibes. Who the devil moved my tapes, here? Don't touch my things, any of you. I won't have it."

"Osden," said Asnanifoil in his large slow voice, "why *are* you such a bastard?"

Ander Eskwana cowered and put his hands in front of his face. Contention frightened him. Olleroo looked up with a vacant yet eager expression, the eternal spectator.

"Why shouldn't I be?" said Osden. He was not looking at Asnanifoil, and was keeping physically as far away from all of them as he could in the crowded cabin. "None of you constitute, in yourselves, any reason for my changing my behavior."

Harfex, a reserved and patient man, said, "The reason is that we shall be spending several years together. Life will be better for all of us if—"

"Can't you understand that I don't give a damn for all of you?" Osden said, took up his microtapes, and went out. Eskwana had suddenly gone to sleep. Asnanifoil was drawing slipstreams in the air with his finger and muttering the Ritual Primes. "You cannot explain his presence on the team except as a plot on the part of the Terran Authority. I saw this almost at once. This mission is meant to fail," Harfex whispered to the Coordinator, glancing over his shoulder. Porlock was fumbling with his fly-button; there were tears in his eyes. I did tell you they were all crazy, but you thought I was exaggerating.

All the same, they were not unjustified. Extreme Surveyors expected to find their fellow team members intelligent, well-trained, unstable, and personally sympathetic. They had to work together in close quarters and nasty places, and could expect one another's paranoias, depressions, manias, phobias and compulsions to be mild enough to admit of good personal relationships, at least most of the time. Osden might be intelligent, but his training was sketchy and his personality was disastrous. He had been sent only on account of his singular gift, the power of empathy: properly speaking, of wide-range bioempathic receptivity. His talent wasn't species-specific; he could pick up emotion or sentience from anything that felt. He could share lust with a white rat, pain with a squashed cockroach, and phototropy with a moth. On an alien world, the Authority had decided, it would be useful to know if anything nearby is sentient, and if so, what its feelings towards you are. Osden's title was a new one: he was the team's Sensor.

"What is emotion, Osden?" Haito Tomiko asked him one day in the main cabin, trying to make some rapport with him for once. "What is it, exactly, that you pick up with your empathic sensitivity?"

"Muck," the man answered in his high, exasperated voice. "The psychic excreta of the animal kingdom. I wade through your feces."

"I was trying," she said, "to learn some facts." She thought her tone was admirably calm.

"You weren't after facts. You were trying to get at me. With some fear, some curiosity, and a great deal of distaste. The way you might poke a dead dog, to see the maggots crawl. Will you understand once and for all that I don't want to be got at, that I want to be left alone?" His skin was mottled with red and violet, his voice had risen. "Go roll in your own dung, you yellow bitch!" he shouted at her silence.

"Calm down," she said, still quietly, but she left him at once and went to her cabin. Of course he had been right about her motives; her question had been largely a pretext, a mere effort to interest him. But what harm in that? Did not that effort imply respect for the other? At the moment of asking the question she had felt at most a slight distrust of him; she had mostly felt sorry for him, the poor arrogant venomous bastard, Mr. No-Skin as Olleroo called him. What did he expect, the way he acted? Love?

"I guess he can't stand anybody feeling sorry for him," said Olleroo, lying on the lower bunk, gilding her nipples.

"Then he can't form any human relationship. All his Dr. Hammergeld did was turn an autism inside out . . ."

"Poor frot," said Olleroo. "Tomiko, you don't mind if Harfex comes in for a while tonight, do you?"

"Can't you go to his cabin? I'm sick of always having to sit in Main with that damned peeled turnip."

"You do hate him, don't you? I guess he feels that. But I slept with Harfex last night too, and Asnanifoil might get jealous, since they share the cabin. It would be nicer here."

"Service them both," Tomiko said with the coarseness of offended modesty. Her Terran subculture, the East Asian, was a puritanical one; she had been brought up chaste.

"I only like one a night," Olleroo replied with innocent serenity. Beldene, the Garden Planet, had never discovered chastity, or the wheel.

"Try Osden, then," Tomiko said. Her personal instability was seldom so plain as now: a profound self-distrust manifesting itself as destructivism. She had volunteered for this job because there was, in all probability, no use in doing it.

The little Beldene looked up, paintbrush in hand, eyes wide. "Tomiko, that was a dirty thing to say."

"Why?"

"It would be vile! I'm not attracted to Osden!"

"I didn't know it mattered to you," Tomiko said indifferently, though she did know. She got some papers together and left the cabin, remarking, "I hope you and Harfex or whoever it is finish by last bell; I'm tired."

Olleroo was crying, tears dripping on her little gilded nipples. She wept easily. Tomiko had not wept since she was ten years old.

It was not a happy ship; but it took a turn for the better when Asnanifoil and his computers raised World 4470. There it lay, a dark-green jewel, like truth at the bottom of a gravity well. As they watched the jade disc grow, a sense of mutuality grew among them. Osden's selfishness, his accurate cruelty, served now to draw the others together. "Perhaps," Mannon said, "he was sent as a beating-gron. What Terrans call a scapegoat. Perhaps his influence will be good after all." And no one, so careful were they to be kind to one another, disagreed.

They came into orbit. There were no lights on nightside, on the continents none of the lines and clots made by animals who build.

"No men," Harfex murmured.

"Of course not," snapped Osden, who had a viewscreen to himself, and his head inside a polythene bag. He claimed that the plastic cut down on the empathic noise he received from the others. "We're two light centuries past the limit of the Hanish Expansion, and outside that there are no men. Anywhere. You don't think Creation would have made the same hideous mistake twice?"

No one was paying him much heed; they were looking with affection at that jade immensity below them, where there was life, but not human life. They were misfits among men, and what they saw there was not desolation, but peace. Even Osden did not look quite so expressionless as usual; he was frowning.

Descent in fire on the sea; air reconnaissance; landing. A plain of something like grass, thick, green, bowing stalks, surrounded the ship, brushed against extended view cameras, smeared the lenses with a fine pollen.

"It looks like a pure phytosphere," Harfex said. "Osden, do you pick up anything sentient?"

They all turned to the Sensor. He had left the screen and was pouring himself a cup of tea. He did not answer. He seldom answered spoken questions.

The chitinous rigidity of military discipline was quite inapplicable to these teams of mad scientists; their chain of command lay somewhere between parliamentary procedure and peck-order, and would have driven a regular service officer out of his mind. By the inscrutable decision of the Authority, however, Dr. Haito Tomiko had been given the title of Coordinator, and she now exercised her prerogative for the first time. "Mr. Sensor Osden," she said, "please answer Mr. Harfex."

"How could I 'pick up' anything from outside," Osden said without turning, "with the emotions of nine neurotic hominids pulsating around me like worms in a can? When I have anything to tell you, I'll tell you. I'm aware of my responsibility as Sensor. If you presume to give me an order again, however, Coordinator Haito, I'll consider my responsibility void."

"Very well, Mr. Sensor. I trust no orders will be needed henceforth." Tomiko's bullfrog voice was calm, but Osden seemed to flinch slightly as he stood with his back to her, as if the surge of her suppressed rancor had struck him with physical force.

The biologist's hunch proved correct. When they began field analyses they found no animals even among the microbiota. Nobody here ate anybody else. All life-forms were photosynthesizing or saprophagous, living off light or death, not off life. Plants: infinite plants, not one species known to the visitors from the house of Man. Infinite shades and intensities of green, violet, purple, brown, red. Infinite silences. Only the wind moved, swaying leaves and fronds, a warm soughing wind laden with spores and pollens, blowing the sweet pale-green dust over prairies of great grasses, heaths that bore no heather, flowerless forests where no foot had ever walked, no eye had ever looked. A warm, sad world, sad and serene. the Surveyors wandering like picknickers over sunny plains of violet filicaliformes, spoke softly to each other. They knew their voices broke a silence of a thousand million years, the silence of wind and leaves, leaves and wind, blowing and ceasing and blowing again. They talked softly; but being human, they talked.

"Poor old Osden," said Jenny Chong, Bio and Tech, as she piloted a helijet on the North Polar Quadrating run. "All that fancy hi-fi stuff in his brain and nothing to receive. What a bust."

"He told me he hates plants," Olleroo said with a giggle.

"You'd think he'd like them, since they don't bother him like we do."

"Can't say I much like these plants myself," said Porlock, looking down at the purple undulations of the North Circumpolar Forest. "All the same. No mind. No change. A man alone in it would go right off his head."

"But it's all alive," Jenny Chong said. "And if it lives, Osden hates it."

"He's not really so bad," Olleroo said, magnanimous.

Porlock looked at her sidelong and asked, "You ever slept with him, Olleroo?" Olleroo burst into tears and cried, "You Terrans are obscene!"

"No she hasn't," Jenny Chong said, prompt to defend. "Have you, Porlock?"

The chemist laughed uneasily: ha, ha, ha. Flecks of spittle appeared on his mustache.

"Osden can't bear to be touched," Olleroo said shakily. "I just brushed against him once by accident and he knocked me off like I was some sort of dirty . . . thing. We're all just things, to him,"

"He's evil," Porlock said in a strained voice, startling the two women. "He'll end up shattering this team, sabotaging it, one way or another. Mark my words. He's not fit to live with other people!" They landed on the North Pole. A midnight sun smoldered over low hills. Short, dry, greenish-pink bryoform grasses stretched away in every direction, which was all one direction, south. Subdued by the incredible silence, the three Surveyors set up their instruments and set to work, three viruses twitching minutely on the hide of an unmoving giant.

Nobody asked Osden along on runs as pilot or photographer or recorder, and he never volunteered, so he seldom left base camp. He ran Harfex's botanical taxonomic data through the onship computers, and served as assistant to Eskwana, whose job here was mainly repair and maintenance. Eskwana had begun to sleep a great deal, twenty-five hours or more out of the thirty-two-hour day, dropping off in the middle of repairing a radio or checking the guidance circuits of a helijet. The Coordinator stayed at base one day to observe. No one else was home except Poswet To, who was subject to epileptic fits; Mannon had plugged her into a therapy-circuit today in a state of preventive catatonia. Tomiko spoke reports into the storage banks, and kept an eye on Osden and Eskwana. Two hours passed.

"You might want to use the 860 microwaldoes in sealing that connection," Eskwana said in his soft, hesitant voice.

"Obviously!"

"Sorry. I just saw you had the 840's there—"

"And will replace them when I take the 860's out. When I

don't know how to proceed, Engineer, I'll ask your advice."

After a minute Tomiko looked round. Sure enough, there was Eskwana sound asleep, head on the table, thumb in his mouth. "Osden."

The white face did not turn, he did not speak, but conveyed impatiently that he was listening.

"You can't be unaware of Eskwana's vulnerability."

"I am not responsible for his psychopathic reactions."

"But you are responsible for your own. Eskwana is essential to our work here, and you're not. If you can't control your hostility, you must avoid him altogether."

Osden put down his tools and stood up. "With pleasure!" he said in his vindictive, scraping voice. "You could not possibly imagine what it's like to experience Eskwana's irrational terrors. To have to share his horrible cowardice, to have to cringe with him at everything!"

"Are you trying to justify your cruelty towards him? I thought you had more self-respect." Tomiko found herself shaking with spite. "If your empathic power really makes you share Ander's misery, why does it never induce the least compassion in you?"

"Compassion," Osden said. "Compassion. What do you know about compassion?"

She stared at him, but he would not look at her.

"Would you like me to verbalize your present emotional affect regarding myself?" he said. "I can do more precisely than you can. I'm trained to analyze such responses as I receive them. And I do receive them."

"But how can you expect me to feel kindly towards you when you behave as you do?"

"What does it matter how I *behave*, you stupid sow, do you think it makes any difference? Do you think the average human is a well of loving-kindness? My choice is to be hated or to be despised. Not being a woman or a coward, I prefer to be hated."

"That's rot. Self-pity. Every man has—"

"But I am not a man," Osden said. "There are all of you. And there is myself. I am *one*."

Awed by that glimpse of abysmal solipsism, she kept silent a while; finally she said with neither spite nor pity, clinically, "You could kill yourself, Osden."

"That's your way, Haito," he jeered. "I'm not depressive, and *seppuku* isn't my bit. What do you want me to do here?"

"Leave. Spare yourself and us. Take the aircar and a data-feeder and go do a species count. In the forest; Harfex hasn't even started the forests yet. Take a hundred-square-meter forested area, anywhere inside radio range. But outside empathy range. Report in at 8 and 24 o'clock daily."

Osden went, and nothing was heard from him for five days but laconic all-well signals twice daily. The mood at base camp changed like a stage-set. Eskwana stayed awake up to eighteen hours a day. Poswet To got her stellar lute and chanted the celestial harmonies (music had driven Osden into a frenzy). Mannon, Harfex, Jenny Chong, and Tomiko all went off tranquilizers. Porlock distilled something in his laboratory and drank it all by himself. He had a hangover. Asnanifoil and Poswet To held an all-night Numerical Epiphany, that mystical orgy of higher mathematics which is the chief pleasure of the religious Cetian soul. Olleroo slept with everybody. Work went well.

The Hard Scientist came towards base at a run, laboring through the high, fleshy stalks of the graminiformes. "Something—in the forest—" His eyes bulged, he panted, his mustache and fingers trembled. "Something big. Moving, behind me. I was putting in a benchmark, bending down. It came at me. As if it was swinging down out of the trees. Behind me." He stared at the others with the opaque eyes of terror or exhaustion.

"Sit down, Porlock. Take it easy. Now wait, go through this again. You *saw* something—"

"Not clearly. Just the movement. Purposive. A—an—I don't know what it could have been. Something self-moving. In the trees, the arboriformes, whatever you call 'em. At the edge of the woods."

Harfex looked grim. "There is nothing here that could attack you, Porlock. There are not even microzoa. There *could not* be a large animal."

"Could you possible have seen an epiphyte drop suddenly, a vine come loose behind you?"

"No," Porlock said. "It was coming down at me, through the branches. When I turned it took off again, away and upward. It made a noise, a sort of crashing. If it wasn't an animal, God knows what it could have been! It was big—as big as a man, at least. Maybe a reddish color. I couldn't see, I'm not sure."

"It was Osden," said Jenny Chong, "doing a Tarzan act." She giggled nervously, and Tomiko repressed a wild feckless laugh. But Harfex was not smiling.

"One gets uneasy under the arboriformes," he said in his polite, repressed voice. "I've noticed that. Indeed that may be why I've put off working in the forests. There's a hypnotic quality in the colors and spacing of the stems and branches, especially the helically-arranged ones; and the spore-throwers grow so regularly spaced that it seems unnatural. I find it quite disagreeable, subjectively speaking. I wonder if a stronger effect of that sort mightn't have produced a hallucination . . . ?"

Porlock shook his head. He wet his lips. "It was there," he said. "Something. Moving with purpose. Trying to attack me from behind."

When Osden called in, punctual as always, at 24 o'clock that night, Harfex told him Porlock's report. "Have you come on anything at all, Mr. Osden, that could substantiate Mr. Porlock's impression of a motile, sentient life-form, in the forest?"

Ssss, the radio said sardonically. "No. Bullshit," said Osden's unpleasant voice.

"You've been actually inside the forest longer than any of us," Harfex said with unmitigable politeness. "Do you agree with my impression that the forest ambiance has a rather troubling and possibly hallucinogenic effect on the perceptions?"

Ssss. "I'll agree that Porlock's perceptions are easily troubled. Keep him in his lab, he'll do less harm. Anything else?"

"Not at present," Harfex said, and Osden cut off.

Nobody could credit Porlock's story, and nobody could discredit it. He was positive that something, something big, had tried to attack him by surprise. It was hard to deny this, for they were on an alien world, and everyone who had entered the forest had felt a certain chill and foreboding under the "trees." ("Call them trees, certainly," Harfex had said. "They really are the same thing, only, of course, altogether different.") They agreed that they had felt uneasy, or had had the sense that something was watching them from behind.

"We've got to clear this up," Porlock said, and he asked to be sent as a temporary Biologist's Aide, like Osden, into the forest to explore and observe. Olleroo and Jenny Chong volunteered if they could go as a pair. Harfex sent them all off into the forest near which they were encamped, a vast tract covering four-fifths of Continent D. He forbade sidearms. They were not to go outside a fifty-mile half-circle, which included Osden's current site. They all reported in twice daily, for three days. Porlock reported a glimpse of what seemed to be a large semi-erect shape moving through the trees across the river; Olleroo was sure she had heard something moving near the tent, the second night.

"There are no animals on this planet," Harfex said, dogged.

Then Osden missed his morning call.

Tomiko waited less than an hour, then flew with Harfex to the area where Osden had reported himself the night before. But as the helijet hovered over the sea of purplish leaves, illimitable, impenetrable, she felt a panic despair. "How can we find him in this?"

"He reported landing on the riverbank. Find the aircar; he'll be camped near it, and he can't have gone far from his camp. Species-counting is slow work. There's the river."

"There's his car," Tomiko said, catching the bright foreign glint among the vegetable colors and shadows. "Here goes, then."

She put the ship in hover and pitched out the ladder. She and Harfex descended. The sea of life closed over their heads.

As her feet touched the forest floor, she unsnapped the flap of her holster; then glancing at Harfex, who was unarmed, she left the gun untouched. But her hand kept coming back to it. There was no sound at all, as soon as they were a few meters away from the slow, brown river, and the light was dim. Great boles stood well apart, almost regularly, almost alike; they were soft-skinned, some appearing smooth and others spongy, grey or greenish-brown or brown, twined with cable-like creepers and festooned with epiphytes, extending rigid, entangled armfuls of big, saucer-shaped, dark leaves that formed a roof-layer twenty to thirty meters thick. The ground underfoot was springy as a mattress, every inch of it knotted with roots and peppered with small, fleshy-leafed growths.

"Here's his tent," Tomiko said, cowed at the sound of her voice in that huge community of the voiceless. In the tent was Osden's sleeping bag, a couple of books, a box of rations. *We should be calling, shouting for him,* she thought, but did not even suggest it; nor did Harfex. They circled out from the tent, careful to keep each other in sight through the thick-standing presences, the crowding gloom. She stumbled over Osden's body, not thirty meters from the tent, led to it by the whitish gleam of a dropped notebook. He lay face down between two huge-rooted trees. His head and hands were covered with blood, some dried, some still oozing red.

Harfex appeared beside her, his pale Hainish complexion quite green in the dusk. "Dead?"

"No. He's been struck. Beaten. From behind." Tomiko's fingers felt over the bloody skull and temples and nape. "A weapon or a tool . . . I don't find a fracture."

As she turned Osden's body over so they could lift him, his eyes opened. She was holding him, bending close to his face. His pale lips writhed. A deathly fear came into her. She screamed aloud two or three times and tried to run away, shambling and stumbling into the terrible dusk. Harfex caught her, and at his touch and the sound of his voice, her panic decreased. "What is it? What is it?" he was saying.

"I don't know," she sobbed. Her heartbeat still shook her, and she could not see clearly. "The fear—the . . . I panicked. When I saw his eyes."

"We're both nervous. I don't understand this—"

"I'm all right now, come on, we've got to get him under care."

Both working with senseless haste, they lugged Osden to the riverside and hauled him up on a rope under his armpits; he dangled like a sack, twisting a little, over the glutinous dark sea of leaves. They pulled him into the helijet and took off. Within a minute they were over open prairie. Tomiko locked onto the homing beam. She drew a deep breath, and her eyes met Harfex's. "I was so terrified I almost fainted. I have never done that."

"I was . . . unreasonably frightened also," said the Hainishman, and indeed he looked aged and shaken. "Not so badly as you. But as unreasonably."

"It was when I was in contact with him, holding him. He seemed to be conscious for a moment."

"Empathy?...I hope he can tell us what attacked him."

Osden, like a broken dummy covered with blood and mud, half lay as they had bundled him into the rear seats in their frantic urgency to get out of the forest.

More panic met their arrival at base. The ineffective brutality of the assault was sinister and bewildering. Since Harfex stubbornly denied any possibility of animal life they began speculating about sentient plants, vegetable monsters, psychic projections. Jenny Chong's latent phobia reasserted itself and she could talk about nothing except the Dark Egos which followed people around behind their backs. She and Olleroo and Porlock had been summoned back to base; and nobody was much inclined to go outside.

Osden had lost a good deal of blood during the three or four hours he had lain alone, and concussion and severe contusions had put him in shock and semi-coma. As he came out of this and began running a low fever he called several times for "Doctor," in a plaintive voice: "Doctor Hammergeld..." When he regained full consciousness, two of those long days later, Tomiko called Harfex into his cubicle.

"Osden: can you tell us what attacked you?"

The pale eyes flickered past Harfex's face.

"You were attacked," Tomiko said gently. The shifty gaze was hatefully familiar, but she was a physician, protective of the hurt. "You may not remember it yet. Something attacked you. You were in the forest—"

"Ah!" he cried out, his eyes growing bright and his features contorting. "The forest—in the forest—"

"What's in the forest?"

He grasped for breath. A look of clearer consciousness came into his face. After a while he said, "I don't know."

"Did you see what attacked you?" Harfex asked.

"I don't know."

"You remember it now."

"I don't know."

"All our lives may depend on this. You must tell us what you saw!"

"I don't know," Osden said, sobbing with weakness. He was too weak to hide the fact that he was hiding the answer, yet he would not say it. Porlock, nearby, was chewing his pepper-colored mustache as he tried to hear what was going on in the cubicle. Harfex leaned over Osden and said, "You *will* tell us—" Tomiko had to interfere bodily.

Harfex controlled himself with an effort that was painful to see. He went off silently to his cubicle, where no doubt he took a double or triple dose of tranquilizers. The other men and women scattered about the big frail building, a long main hall and ten sleeping-cubicles, said nothing, but looked depressed and edgy. Osden, as always, even now, had them all at his mercy. Tomiko looked down at him with a rush of hatred that burned in her throat like bile. This monstrous egotism that fed itself on others' emotions, this absolute selfishness, was worse than any hideous deformity of the flesh. Like a congenital monster, he should not have lived. Should not be alive. Should have died. Why had his head not been split open?

As he lay flat and white, his hands helpless at his sides, his colorless eyes were wide open, and there were tears running from the corners. He tried to flinch away. "Don't," he said in a weak hoarse voice, and tried to raise his hands to protect his head. "Don't!"

She sat down on the folding-stool beside the cot, and after a while put her hand on his. He tried to pull away, but lacked the strength.

A long silence fell between them.

"Osden," she murmured, "I'm sorry. I'm very sorry. I will you well. Let me will you well, Osden. I don't want to hurt you. Listen, I do see now. It was one of us. That's right, isn't it. No, don't answer, only tell me if I'm wrong; but I'm not ... Of course there are animals on this planet. Ten of them. I don't care who it was. It doesn't matter, does it. It could have been me, just now. I realize that. I didn't understand how it is, Osden. You can't see how difficult it is for us to understand ... But listen. If it were love, instead of hate and fear ... It is never love?"

"No."

"Why not? Why should it never be? Are human beings all so weak? That is terrible. Never mind, never mind, don't worry. Keep still. At least right now it isn't hate, is it? Sympathy at least, concern, well-wishing, you do feel that, Osden? Is it what you feel?"

"Among ... other things," he said, almost inaudibly.

"Noise from my subconscious, I suppose. And everybody else in the room ... Listen, when we found you there in the forest, when I tried to turn you over, you partly wakened, and I felt a horror of you. I was insane with fear for a minute. Was that your fear of me I felt?"

"No."

Her hand was still on his, and he was quite relaxed, sinking towards sleep, like a man in pain who has been given relief from pain. "The forest," he muttered; she could barely understand him. "Afraid."

She pressed him no further, but kept her hand on his and watched him go to sleep. She knew what she felt, and what therefore he must feel. She was confident of it: there is only one emotion, or state of being, that can thus wholly reverse itself, polarize, within one moment. In Great Hainish indeed there is one word, *onta*, for love and for hate. She was not in love with Osden, of course, that was another kettle of fish. What she felt for him was *onta*, polarized hate. She held his hand and the current flowed between them, the tremendous electricity of touch, which he had always dreaded. As he slept the ring of anatomy-chart muscles around his mouth relaxed, and Tomiko saw on his face what none of them had ever seen, very faint, a smile. It faded. He slept on.

He was tough; next day he was sitting up, and hungry. Harfex wished to interrogate him, but Tomiko put him off. She hung a sheet of polythene over the cubicle door, as Osden himself had often done. "Does it actually cut down your empathic reception?" she asked, and he replied, in the dry, cautious tone they were now using to each other, "No."

"Just a warning, then."

"Partly. More faith-healing. Dr. Hammergeld thought it worked . . . Maybe it does, a little."

There had been love, once. A terrified child, suffocating in the tidal rush and battering of the huge emotions of adults, a drowning child, saved by one man. Taught to breathe, to live, by one man. Given everything, all protection and love, by one man. Father/Mother/God: no other. "Is he still alive?" Tomiko asked, thinking of Osden's incredible loneliness, and the strange cruelty of the great doctors. She was shocked when she heard his forced, tinny laugh. "He died at least two and a half centuries ago," Osden said. "Do you forget where we are, Coordinator? We've all left our little families behind . . ."

Outside the polythene curtain the eight other human beings on World 4470 moved vaguely. Their voices were low and strained. Eskwana slept; Poswet To was in therapy; Jenny Chong was trying to rig lights in her cubicle so that she wouldn't cast a shadow.

"They're all scared," Tomiko said, scared. "They've all got these ideas about what attacked you. A sort of ape-potato, a giant fanged spinach, I don't know . . . Even Harfex. You may be right not to force them to see. That would be worse, to lose confidence in one another. But why are we all so shaky, unable to face the fact, going to pieces so easily? Are we really all insane?"

"We'll soon be more so."

"Why?"

"There *is* something." He closed his mouth, the muscles of his lips stood out rigid.

"Something sentient?"

"A sentience."

"In the forest?" He nodded.

"What is it, then—?"

"The fear." He began to look strained again, and moved restlessly. "When I fell, there, you know, I didn't lose consciousness at once. Or I kept regaining it. I don't know. It was more like being paralyzed."

"You were."

"I was on the ground. I couldn't get up. My face was in the dirt, in that soft leaf mold. It was in my nostrils and eyes. I couldn't move. Couldn't see. As if I was in the ground. Sunk into it, part of it. I knew I was between two trees even though I never saw them. I suppose I could feel the roots. Below me in the ground, down under the ground. My hands were bloody, I could feel that, and the blood made the dirt around my face sticky. I felt the fear. It kept growing. As if they'd finally *known* I was there, lying on them there, under them, among them, the thing they feared, and yet part of their fear itself. I couldn't stop sending the fear back, and it kept growing, and I couldn't move, I couldn't get away. I would pass out, I think, and then the fear would bring me to again, and I still couldn't move. Any more than they can."

Tomiko felt the cold stirring of her hair, the readying of the apparatus of terror. "They: who are they, Osden?"

"They, it—I don't know. The fear."

"What is he talking about?" Harfex demanded when Tomiko reported this conversation. She would not let Harfex question Osden yet, feeling that she must protect Osden from the onslaught of the Hainishman's powerful, over-repressed emotions. Unfortunately this fueled the slow fire of paranoid anxiety that burned in poor Harfex, and he thought she and Osden were in league, hiding some fact of great importance or peril from the rest of the team.

"It's like the blind man trying to describe the elephant. Osden hasn't seen or heard the . . . the sentience, any more than we have."

"But he's felt it, my dear Haito," Harfex said with just-suppressed rage. "Not empathically. On his skull. It came and knocked him down and beat him with a blunt instrument. Did he not catch *one* glimpse of it?"

"What would he have seen, Harfex?" Tomiko said, but he would not hear her meaningful tone; even he had blocked out that comprehension. What one fears is alien. The murderer is an outsider, a foreigner, not one of us. The evil is not in me!

"The first blow knocked him pretty well out," Tomiko said a little wearily, "he didn't see anything. But when he came to again, alone in the forest, he felt a great fear. Not his own fear; an empathic effect. He is certain of that. And certain it was nothing picked up from any of us. So that evidently the native life-forms are not all insentient."

Harfex looked at her a moment, grim. "You're trying to frighten me, Haito. I do not understand your motives." He got up and went off to his laboratory table, walking slowly and stiffly, like a man of eighty not of forty.

She looked around at the others. She felt some desperation. Her new, fragile, and profound interdependence with Osden gave her, she was well aware, some added strength. But if even Harfex could not keep his head, who of the others would? Porlock and Eskwana were shut in their cubicles, the others were all working or busy with something. There was something queer about their positions. For a while the Coordinator could not tell what it was, then she saw that they were all sitting facing the nearby forest. Playing chess with Asnanifoil, Olleroo had edged her chair around until it was almost beside his.

She went to Mannon, who was dissecting a tangle of spidery brown roots, and told him to look for the pattern-puzzle. He saw it at once, and said with unusual brevity, "Keeping an eye on the enemy."

"What enemy? What do *you* feel, Mannon?" She had a sudden hope in him as a psychologist, on this obscure ground of hints and empathies where biologists went astray.

"I feel a strong anxiety with a specific spatial orientation. But I am not an empath. Therefore the anxiety is explicable in terms of the particular stress-situation, that is, the attack on a team member in the forest, and also in terms of the total stress-situation, that is, my presence in a totally alien environment, for which the archetypical connotations of the word 'forest' provide an inevitable metaphor."

Hours later Tomiko woke to hear Osden screaming in nightmare; Mannon was calming him, and she sank back into her own dark-branching pathless dreams. In the morning Eskwana did not wake. He could not be roused with stimulant drugs. He clung to his sleep, slipping farther and farther back, mumbling softly now and then until, wholly regressed, he lay curled on his side, thumb at his lips, gone.

"Two days; two down. Ten little Indians, nine little Indians..." That was Porlock.

"And you're the next little Indian," Jenny Chong snapped. "Go analyze your urine, Porlock!"

"He is driving us all insane," Porlock said, getting up and waving his left arm. "Can't you feel it? For God's sake, are you all deaf and blind? Can't you feel what he's doing, the emanations? It all comes from him—from his room there—from his mind. He is driving us all insane with fear!"

"Who is?" said Asnanifoil, looming precipitous and hairy over the little Terran.

"Do I have to say his name? Osden, then. Osden! Osden! Why do you think I tried to kill him? In self-defense! To save all of us! Because you won't see what he's doing to us. He's sabotaged the mission by making us quarrel, and now he's going to drive us all insane by projecting fear at us so that we can't sleep or think, like a huge radio that doesn't make any sound, but it broadcasts all the time, and you can't sleep, and you can't think. Haito and Harfex are already under his control but the rest of you can be saved. I had to do it!"

"You didn't do it very well," Osden said, standing half-naked, all rib and bandage, at the door of his cubicle. "I could have hit myself harder. Hell, it isn't me that's scaring you blind, Porlock, it's out there—there, in the woods!"

Porlock made an ineffectual attempt to assault Osden; Asnanifoil held him back, and continued to hold him effortlessly while Mannon gave him a sedative shot. He was put away shouting about giant radios. In a minute the sedative took effect, and he joined a peaceful silence to Eskwana's.

"All right," said Harfex. "Now, Osden, you'll tell us what you know and all you know."

Osden said, "I don't know anything."

He looked battered and faint. Tomiko made him sit down before he talked.

"After I'd been three days in the forest, I thought I was occasionally receiving some kind of affect."

"Why didn't you report it?"

"Thought I was going spla, like the rest of you."

"That, equally, should have been reported."

"You'd have called me back to base. I couldn't take it. You realize that my inclusion in the mission was a bad mistake. I'm not able to coexist with nine other neurotic personalities at close quarters. I was wrong to volunteer for Extreme Survey, and the Authority was wrong to accept me."

No one spoke; but Tomiko saw, with certainty this time, the flinch in Osden's shoulders and the tightening of his facial muscles, as he registered their bitter agreement.

"Anyhow, I didn't want to come back to base because I was curious. Even going psycho, how could I pick up empathic effects when there was no creature to emit them? They weren't bad, then. Very vague. Queer. Like a draft in a closed room, a flicker in the corner of your eye. Nothing really."

For a moment he had been borne up on their listening: they heard, so he spoke. He was wholly at their mercy. If they disliked him he had to be hateful; if they mocked him he became grotesque; if they listened to him he was the storyteller. He was helplessly obedient to the demands of their emotions, reactions, moods. And there were seven of them, too many to cope with, so that he must be constantly knocked about from one to another's whim. He could not find coherence. Even as he spoke and held them, some- body's attention would wander: Olleroo perhaps was think- ing that he wasn't unattractive, Harfex was seeking the ulterior motive of his words, Asnanifoil's's mind, which could not be long held by the concrete, was roaming off towards the eternal peace of number, and Tomiko was distracted by pity, by fear. Osden's voice faltered. He lost the thread. "I . . . I thought it must be the trees," he said, and stopped.

"It's not the trees," Harfex said. "They have no more nervous system than do plants of the Hainish Descent on Earth. None."

"You're not seeing the forest for the trees, as they say on Earth," Mannon put in, smiling elfinly; Harfex stared at him. "What about those root-nodes we've been puzzling about for twenty days—eh?"

"What about them?"

"They are, indubitably, connections. Connections among the trees. Right? Now let's just suppose, most improbably, that you knew nothing of animal brain-structure. And you were given one axon, or one detached glial cell, to examine. Would you be likely to discover what it was? Would you see that the cell was capable of sentience?"

"No. Because it isn't. A single cell is capable of mechanical response to stimulus. No more. Are you hypothesizing that individual arboriformes are 'cells' in a kind of brain, Mannon?"

"Not exactly. I'm merely pointing out that they are all interconnected, both by the root-node linkage and by your green epiphytes in the branches. A linkage of incredible complexity and physical extent. Why, even the prairie grassforms have those root-connectors, don't they? I know that sentience or intelligence isn't a thing, you can't find it in, or analyze it out from, the cells of a brain. It's a function of the connected cells. It is, in a sense, the connection: the connectedness. It doesn't exist. I'm not trying to say it exists. I'm only guessing that Osden might be able to describe it."

And Osden took him up, speaking as if in trance. "Sentience without senses. Blind, deaf, nerveless, moveless. Some irritability, response to touch. Response to sun, to light, to water, and chemicals in the earth around the roots. Nothing comprehensible to an animal mind. Presence without mind. Awareness of being, without object or subject. Nirvana."

"Then why do you receive fear?" Tomiko asked in a low voice.

"I don't know. I can't see how awareness of objects, of others, could arise: an unperceiving response . . . But there was an uneasiness, for days. And then when I lay between the two trees and my blood was on their roots—" Osden's face glittered with sweat. "It became fear," he said shrilly, "only fear."

"If such a function existed," Harfex said, "it would not be capable of conceiving of a self-moving, material entity, or responding to one. It could no more become aware of us than we can 'become aware' of Infinity."

" 'The silence of those infinite expanses terrifies me,' " muttered Tomiko. "Pascal was aware of Infinity. By way of fear."

"To a forest," Mannon said, "we might appear as forest fires. Hurricanes. Dangers. What moves quickly is dangerous, to a plant. The rootless would be alien, terrible. And if it is mind, it seems only too probable that it might become aware of Osden, whose own mind is open to connection with all others so long as he's conscious, and who was lying in pain and afraid within it, actually inside it. No wonder it was afraid—"

"Not 'it,'" Harfex said. "There is no being, no huge creature, no person! There could at most be only a function—"

"There is only a fear," Osden said.

They were all still a while, and heard the stillness outside.

"Is that what I feel all the time coming up behind me?" Jenny Chong asked, subdued.

Osden nodded. "You all feel it, deaf as you are. Eskwana's the worst off, because he actually has some empathic capacity. He could send if he learned how, but he's too weak, never will be anything but a medium."

"Listen, Osden," Tomiko said, "you can send. Then send to it—the forest, the fear out there—tell it that we won't hurt it. Since it has, or is, some sort of affect that translates into what we feel as emotion, can't you translate back? Send out a message, We are harmless, we are friendly."

"You must know that nobody can emit a false empathic message, Haito. You can't send something that doesn't exist."

"But we don't intend harm, we are friendly."

"Are we? In the forest, when you picked me up, did you feel friendly?"

"No. Terrified. But that's—it, the forest, the plants, not my own fear, isn't it?"

"What's the difference? It's all you felt. Can't you see," and Osden's voice rose in exasperation, "why I dislike you and you dislike me, all of you? Can't you see that I retransmit every negative or aggressive affect you've felt towards me since we first met? I return your hostility, with thanks. I do it in self-defense. Like Porlock. It is self-defense, though; it's the only technique I developed to replace my original defense of total withdrawal from others. Unfortunately it creates a closed circuit, self-sustaining and self-reinforcing. Your initial reaction to me was the instinctive antipathy to a cripple; by now of course it's hatred. Can you fail to see my point? The forest mind out there transmits only terror, now, and the only message I can send it is terror, because when exposed to it I can feel nothing except terror!"

"What must we do, then?" said Tomiko, and Mannon replied promptly, "Move camp. To another continent. If there are plant-minds there, they'll be slow to notice us, as this one was; maybe they won't notice us at all."

"It would be a considerable relief," Osden observed stiffly. The others had been watching him with a new curiosity. He had revealed himself, they had seen him as he was, a helpless man in a trap. Perhaps, like Tomiko, they had seen that the trap itself, his crass and cruel egotism, was their own construction, not his. They had built the cage and locked him in it, and like a caged ape he threw filth out through the bars. If, meeting him, they had offered trust, if they had been strong enough to offer him love, how might he have appeared to them?

None of them could have done so, and it was too late

now. Given time, given solitude, Tomiko might have built up with him a slow resonance of feeling, a consonance of trust, a harmony; but there was no time, their job must be done. There was not room enough for the cultivation of so great a thing, and they must make do with sympathy, with pity, the small change of love. Even that much had given her strength, but it was nowhere near enough for him. She could see in his flayed face now his savage resentment of their curiosity, even of her pity.

"Go lie down, that gash is bleeding again," she said, and he obeyed her.

Next morning they packed up, melted down the spray-form hangar and living quarters, lifted *Gum* on mechanical drive and took her halfway round World 4470, over the red and green lands, the many warm green seas. They had picked out a likely spot on continent G: a prairie, twenty thousand square kilos of windswept graminiformes. No forest was within a hundred kilos of the site, and there were no lone trees or groves on the plain. The plant-forms occurred only in large species-colonies, never intermingled, except for certain tiny ubiquitous saprophytes and spore-bearers. The team sprayed holomeld over structure forms, and by evening of the thirty-two-hour day were settled in to the new camp. Eskwana was still asleep and Porlock still sedated, but everyone else was cheerful. "You can breathe here!" they kept saying.

Osden got on his feet and went shakily to the doorway; leaning there he looked through twilight over the dim reaches of the swaying grass that was not grass. There was a faint, sweet odor of pollen on the wind; no sound but the soft, vast sibilance of wind. His bandaged head cocked a little, the empath stood motionless for a long time. Darkness came, and the stars, lights in the windows of the distant house of Man. The wind had ceased, there was no sound. He listened.

In the long night Haito Tomiko listened. She lay still and heard the blood in her arteries, the breathing of sleepers, the wind blowing, the dark veins running, the dreams advancing, the vast static of stars increasing as the universe died slowly, the sound of death walking. She struggled out of her bed, fled the tiny solitude of her cubicle. Eskwana alone slept. Porlock lay straitjacketed, raving softly in his obscure native tongue. Olleroo and Jenny Chong were playing cards, grim-faced. Poswet To was in the therapy niche, plugged in. Asnanifoil was drawing a mandala, the Third Pattern of the Primes. Mannon and Harfex were sitting up with Osden.

She changed the bandages on Osden's head. His lank, reddish hair, where she had not had to shave it, looked strange. It was salted with white, now. Her hands shook as she worked. Nobody had yet said anything.

"How can the fear be here too?" she said, and her voice rang flat and false in the terrific silence.

"It's not just the trees; the grasses..."

"But we're twelve thousand kilos from where we were this morning, we left it on the other side of the planet."

"It's all one," Osden said. "One big green thought. How long does it take a thought to get from one side of your brain to the other?"

"It doesn't think. It isn't thinking," Harfex said, lifelessly. "It's merely a network of processes. The branches, the epiphytic growths, the roots with those nodal junctures between individuals: they must all be capable of transmitting electrochemical impulses. There are no individual plants, then, properly speaking. Even the pollen is part of the linkage, no doubt, a sort of windborne sentience, connecting overseas. But it is not conceivable. That all the biosphere of a planet should be one network of communications, sensitive, irrational, immortal, isolated..."

"Isolated," said Osden. "That's it! That's the fear. It isn't that we're motile, or destructive. It's just that we are. We are other. There has never been any other."

"You're right," Mannon said, almost whispering. "It has no peers. No enemies. No relationship with anything but itself. One alone forever."

"Then what's the function of its intelligence in species-survival?"

"None, maybe," Osden said. "Why are you getting teleological, Harfex? Aren't you a Hainishman? Isn't the measure of complexity the measure of the eternal joy?"

Harfex did not take the bait. He looked ill. "We should leave this world," he said.

"Now you know why I always want to get out, get away from you," Osden said with a kind of morbid geniality. "It isn't pleasant, is it—the other's fear . . . ? If only it were an animal intelligence. I can get through to animals. I get along with cobras and tigers; superior intelligence gives one the advantage. I should have been used in a zoo, not on a human team . . . If I could get through to the damned stupid potato! If it wasn't so overwhelming . . . I still pick up more than the fear, you know. And before it panicked it had a—there was a serenity. I couldn't take it in, then, I didn't realize how big it was. To know the whole daylight, after all, and the whole night. All the winds and lulls together. The winter stars and the summer stars at the same time. To have roots, and no enemies. To be entire. Do you see? No invasion. No others. To be whole . . ."

He had never spoken before, Tomiko thought.

"You are defenseless against it, Osden," she said. "Your personality has changed already. You're vulnerable to it. We may not all go mad, but you will, if we don't leave."

He hesitated, then he looked up at Tomiko, the first time he had ever met her eyes, a long, still look, clear as water.

What's sanity ever done for me?" he said, mocking. "But you have a point, Haito. You have something there."

"We should get away," Harfex muttered.

"If I gave in to it," Osden mused, "could I communicate?"

"By 'give in,' " Mannon said in a rapid, nervous voice, "I assume that you mean, stop sending back the empathic information which you receive from the plant-entity: stop rejecting the fear, and absorb it. That will either kill you at once, or drive you back into total psychological withdrawal, autism."

"Why?" said Osden. "Its message is *rejection*. But my salvation is rejection. It's not intelligent. But I am."

"The scale is wrong. What can a single human brain achieve against something so vast?"

"A single human brain can perceive pattern on the scale of stars and galaxies," Tomiko said, "and interpret it as Love."

Mannon looked from one to the other of them; Harfex was silent.

"It'd be easier in the forest," Osden said. "Which of you will fly me over?"

"When?"

"Now. Before you all crack up or go violent."

"I will," Tomiko said.

"None of us will," Harfex said.

"I can't," Mannon said. "I . . . I am too frightened. I'd crash the jet."

"Bring Eskwana along. If I can pull this off, he might serve as a medium."

"Are you accepting the Sensor's plan, Coordinator?" Harfex asked formally.

"Yes."

"I disapprove. I will come with you, however."

"I think we're compelled, Harfex," Tomiko said, looking at Osden's face, the ugly white mask transfigured, eager as a lover's face.

Olleroo and Jenny Chong, playing cards to keep their

thoughts from their haunted beds, their mounting dread, chattered like scared children. "This thing, it's in the forest, it'll get you—"

"Scared of the dark?" Osden jeered.

"But look at Eskwana, and Porlock, and even Asnanifoil—"

"It can't hurt you. It's an impulse passing through synapses, a wind passing through branches. It is only a nightmare."

They took off in a helijet, Eskwana curled up still sound asleep in the rear compartment, Tomiko piloting, Harfex and Osden silent, watching ahead for the dark line of the forest across the vague grey miles of starlit plain. They neared the black line, crossed it; now under them was darkness.

She sought a landing place, flying low, though she had to fight her frantic wish to fly high, to get out, get away. The huge vitality of the plant-world was far stronger here in the forest, and its panic beat in immense dark waves. There was a pale patch ahead, a bare knoll-top a little higher than the tallest of the black shapes around it; the not-trees; the rooted; the parts of the whole. She set the helijet down in the glade, a bad landing. Her hands on the stick were slippery, as if she had rubbed them with cold soap.

About them now stood the forest, black in darkness.

Tomiko cowered and shut her eyes. Eskwana moaned in his sleep. Harfex's breath came short and loud, and he sat rigid, even when Osden reached across him and slid the door open.

Osden stood up; his back and bandaged head were just visible in the dim glow of the control panel as he paused stooping in the doorway.

Tomiko was shaking. She could not raise her head. "No, no, no, no, no, no, no," she said in a whisper. "No. No. No."

Osden moved suddenly and quietly, swinging out of the doorway, down into the dark. He was gone.

I am coming! said a great voice that made no sound.

Tomiko screamed. Harfex coughed; he seemed to be trying to stand up, but did not do so.

Tomiko drew in upon herself, all centered in the blind eye in her belly, in the center of her being; and outside that there was nothing but the fear.

It ceased.

She raised her head; slowly unclenched her hands. She sat up straight. The night was dark, and stars shone over the forest. There was nothing else.

"Osden," she said, but her voice would not come. She spoke again, louder, a lone bullfrog croak. There was no reply.

She began to realize that something had gone wrong with Harfex. She was trying to find his head in the darkness, for he had slipped down from the seat, when all at once, in the dead quiet, in the dark rear compartment of the craft, a voice spoke. "Good," it said. It was Eskwana's voice. She snapped on the interior lights and saw the engineer lying curled up asleep, his hand half over his mouth.

The mouth opened and spoke. "All well," it said.

"Osden—"

"All well," said the voice from Eskwana's mouth.

"Where are you?"

Silence.

"Come back."

A wind was rising. "I'll stay here," the soft voice said.

"You can't stay—"

Silence.

"You'd be alone, Osden!"

"Listen." The voice was fainter, slurred, as if lost in the sound of wind. "Listen. I will you well."

She called his name after that, but there was no answer. Eskwana lay still. Harfex lay stiller.

"Osden!" she cried, leaning out the doorway into the

dark, wind-shaken silence of the forest of being. "I will come back. I must get Harfex to the base. I will come back, Osden!"

Silence and wind in leaves.

They finished the prescribed survey of World 4470, the eight of them; it took them forty-one days more Asnanifoil and one or another of the women went into the forest daily at first, searching for Osden in the region around the bare knoll, though Tomiko was not in her heart sure which bare knoll they had landed on that night in the very heart and vortex of terror. They left piles of supplies for Osden, food enough for fifty years, clothing, tents, tools. They did not go on searching; there was no way to find a man alone, hiding, if he wanted to hide, in those unending labyrinths and dim corridors vine-entangled, root-floored. They might have passed within arm's reach of him and never seen him.

But he was there; for there was no fear any more. Rational, and valuing reason more highly after an intolerable experience of the immortal mindless, Tomiko tried to understand rationally what Osden had done. But the words escaped her control. He had taken the fear into himself, and, accepting, had transcended it. He had given up his self to the alien, an unreserved surrender, that left no place for evil. He had learned the love of the Other, and thereby had been given his whole self.—But this is not the vocabulary of reason.

The people of the Survey team walked under the trees, through the vast colonies of life, surrounded by a dreaming silence, a brooding calm that was half aware of them and wholly indifferent to them. There were no hours. Distance was no matter. Had we but world enough and time... The planet turned between the sunlight and the great dark; winds of winter and summer blew fine, pale pollen across the quiet seas.

Gum returned after many surveys, years, and lightyears, to what had several centuries ago been Smeming Port. There were still men there, to receive (incredulously) the team's reports, and to record its losses: Biologist Harfex, dead of fear, and Sensor Osden, left as a colonist.

(1971)

VI

Seven Bird and Beast Poems

Various real or imaginary relations and comminglings of human and other beings are going on here. The last one is a true ghost story.

*The first one is a joke about one of my favorite kinds of bird, the acorn woodpecker (*Melanerpes formicivorus *in* Latin, boso *in* Kesh*). They are handsome little woodpeckers, still common in Northern California, splendidly marked, with a red cap, and a white circle round the eye giving them a clown's mad stare. They talk all the time—the loud yacka-yacka-yacka call, and all kinds of mutters, whirs, purrs, comments, criticisms, and gossip going on constantly among the foraging or housekeeping group. They are familial or tribal. Cousins and aunts help a mated pair feed and bring up the babies. Why they make holes and drop acorns into them when they can't get the acorns back out of the holes is still a question (to ornithologists—not to acorn woodpeckers). When we removed the wasp- and woodpecker-riddled back outer wall of an old California farmhouse last year, about a ton of acorns fell out, all worm-hollowed husks; they had never been accessible to the generations of Bosos who had been diligently dropping them in since 1870 or so. But in the walls of the barn are neat rows of little holes, each one with a long Valley Oak acorn stuck in, a perfect fit, almost like rivets in sheet iron. These, presumably, are winter supply. On the other hand, they might be a woodpecker art form. Another funny thing they do is in spring, very early in the morning, when a male wants to assert the tribal territory and/or impress the hell out of some redhead.*

He finds a tree that makes a really loud sound, and drums on it. The loudest tree these days—a fine example of the interfacing of human and woodpecker cultures—is a metal chimney sticking up from a farmhouse roof. A woodpecker doing the kettledrum reveille on the stovepipe is a real good way to start the day at attention.

What is Going on in The Oaks Around the Barn

The Acorn Woodpeckers
are constructing an Implacable
Pecking Machine to attack oaks
and whack holes to stack acorns in.

They have not perfected
it yet. They keep cranking
it up ratchet by ratchet
by ratchet each morning
till a Bluejay yells, "SCRAP!"
and it all collapses
into black-and-white flaps and flutters
and redheads muttering curses
in the big, protecting branches.

(1986)

For Ted

The hawk shapes the wind
and the curve of the wind

Like eggs lie the great gold hills
in the curve of the world
to that keen eye

The children wait

The hawk declares height
by his fell fall

The children cry

Comes the high hunter
carrying the kill
curving the winds
with strong wings

To the old hawk
all earth is prey, and child

(1973)

Found Poem

However, Bruce Baird, Laguna Beach's chief lifeguard, doubts that sea lions could ever replace, or even really aid, his staff. "If you were someone from Ohio, and you were in the water having trouble and a sea lion approached you, well, it would require a whole lot more public education," he told the Orange County Register.
—PAUL SIMON, for AP, 17 December 1984

If I am ever someone from Ohio
in the water having trouble
off a continent's west edge
and am translated to my element
by a sudden warm great animal
with sea-dark fur sleek shining
and the eyes of Shiva,
I hope to sink my troubles like a stone
and all uneducated ride
her inshore shouting with the foam
praises of the freedom to be saved.

(1986)

Totem

Mole my totem
mound builder
maze maker
tooth at the root
shaper of darkness
into ways and hollows

in grave alive
heavy handed
light blinded

(1979)

Winter Downs

(For Barbara)

Eyes look at you.
Thorns catch at you.
Heart starts and bleats.

The looks are rocks
white-ringed with chalk:
flint fish-eyes of old seas,
sheep's flint-dark gaze.

Chalk is sheep-white.
Clouds take shape
and quiet of sheep.
Thorn's hands hold stolen fleece.
The stones sleep open-eyed.

Keep watch: be not afraid.

(1980)

The Man Eater

They'd all run away then.
We came out of the hovels
by the well to wait
as that one came soft
from the branched dark
into the moon-round singing
to wear garlands
by children woven, given
An old one of us

(1986)

brought the goat out
fed well, also garlanded,
but that one ignored
the goat and cast about
among huts and gardens
hunting, hunting.
"They're gone," we sang
while the children
let the goat go.
"They ran away,"
we sang, dancing,
dancing hunting
with that one, with her
who is branched with darkness
and shining,
and is not afraid.

(1986)

Sleeping Out

Don't turn on the flashlight, we won't see
what's crashing its way slow
down there in the foggy darkness
thickening the air with a smell
like wet deadness smoldering,
or why the crickets went still
and coyotes giggle behind the hill.
The light will make a hole
in the air and what we fear
will be more there all round
it in the dark brush and the old dark mind.

(1985)

VII

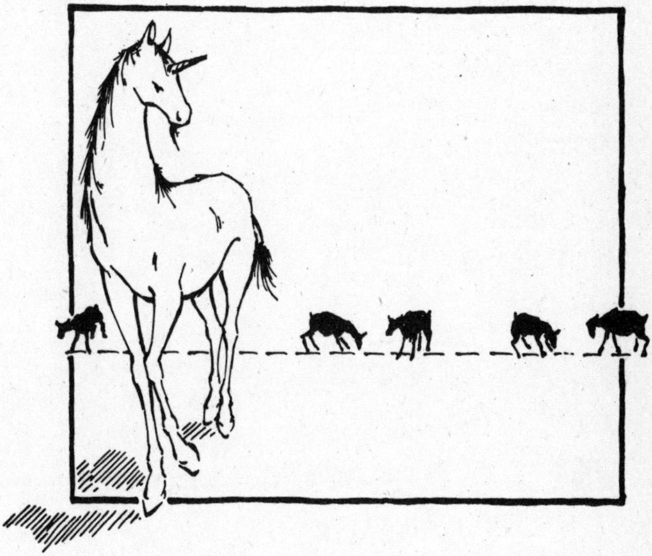

"The White Donkey" and "Horse Camp"

In these two stories, the relationship is that natural, universal, and mysterious one between the child and the animal.

"The White Donkey" was written in the white-hot dawn of a summer morning during the Writers Conference at Indiana University. I had asked the writers in my workshop to write a "last contact" story—"first contact" is a very common theme in science fiction, of which the films Close Encounters of the Third Kind *and* E.T. *are trivial but familiar examples. This story, however, is not science fiction but fantasy, since the creature in question is not an 'alien' or an extra-terrestrial, but just the opposite. It is an animal whose habitat is restricted to the human imagination. Even there it flourishes only within the Western European ecosystem, where a few years ago it experienced quite a population explosion, reproducing itself all over greeting cards, posters, book covers, and other curious ecological niches. But to the child in this story, no recognition is possible.*

"Horse Camp" seems to trouble people, even some who have gone through, or had daughters go through, the "horse stage." Perhaps what troubles them is that one can hear in it a yell of freedom and a scream from the trap in the same voice at the same time. Or maybe they just want to know how. *I don't know.*

The White Donkey

THERE WERE SNAKES IN THE OLD STONE PLACE, but the grass grew so green and rank there that she brought the goats back every day. "The goats are looking fat," Nana said. "Where are you grazing them, Sita?" And when Sita said, "At the old stone place, in the forest," Nana said, "It's a long way to take them," and Uncle Hira said, "Look out for snakes in that place," but they were thinking of the goats, not of her: so she did not ask them, after all, about the white donkey.

She had seen the donkey first when she was putting flowers on the red stone under the pipal tree at the edge of the forest. She liked that stone. It was the Goddess, very old, round, sitting comfortably among the roots of the tree. Everybody who passed by there left the Goddess some flowers or poured a bit of water on her, and every spring her red paint was renewed. Sita was giving the Goddess a rhododendron flower when she looked round, thinking one of the goats was straying off into the forest; but it wasn't a goat. It was a white animal that had caught her eye, whiter than a Brahminee bull. Sita followed, to see what it was. When she saw the neat round rump and the tail like a rope with a tassel, she knew it was a donkey; but such a beautiful donkey! And whose? There were three donkeys in the village, and Chandra Bose owned two, all of them grey, bony, mournful, laborious beasts. This was a tall, sleek, delicate donkey, a wonderful donkey. It could not belong to Chandra Bose, or to anybody in the village, or to anybody in the other village. It wore no halter or harness. It must be wild; it must live in the forest alone.

Sure enough, when she brought the goats along by whistling to clever Kala, and followed where the white donkey had gone into the forest, first there was a path, and then they came to the place where the old stones were, blocks of stone as big as houses all half-buried and overgrown with grass and kerala vines; and there the white donkey was standing looking back at her from the darkness under the trees.

She thought then that the donkey was a god, because it had a third eye in the middle of its forehead like Shiva. But when it turned she saw that that was not an eye, but a horn—not curved like a cow's or a goat's horns, a straight spike like a deer's—just the one horn, between the eyes, like Shiva's eye. So it might be a kind of god donkey; and in case it was, she picked a yellow flower off the kerala vine and offered it, stretching out her open palm.

The white donkey stood a while considering her and the goats and the flower; then it came slowly back among the big stones towards her. It had split hooves like the goats, and walked even more neatly than they did. It accepted the flower. Its nose was pinkish-white, and very soft where it snuffled on Sita's palm. She quickly picked another flower, and the donkey accepted it too. But when she wanted to stroke its face around the short, white, twisted horn and the white, nervous ears, it moved away, looking sidelong at her from its long dark eyes.

Sita was a little afraid of it, and thought it might be a little afraid of her; so she sat down on one of the half-buried rocks and pretended to be watching the goats, who were all busy grazing on the best grass they had had for months. Presently the donkey came close again, and standing beside Sita, rested its curly-bearded chin on her lap. The breath from its nostrils moved the thin glass bangles on her wrist. Slowly and very gently she stroked the base of the white, nervous ears, the fine, harsh hair at the base of the horn, the silken muzzle; and the white donkey stood beside her, breathing long, warm breaths.

Every day since then she brought the goats there, walking carefully because of snakes; and the goats were getting fat; and her friend the donkey came out of the forest every day, and accepted her offering, and kept her company.

"One bullock and one hundred rupees cash," said Uncle Hira, "you're crazy if you think we can marry her for less!"

"Moti Lal is a lazy man," Nana said. "Dirty and lazy."

"Se he wants a wife to work and clean for him! And he'll take her for only one bullock and one hundred rupees cash!"

"Maybe he'll settle down when he's married," Nana said.

So Sita was betrothed to Moti Lal from the other village, who had watched her driving the goats home at evening. She had seen him watching her across the road, but had never looked at him. She did not want to look at him.

"This is the last day," she said to the white donkey, while the goats cropped the grass among the big, carved, fallen stones, and the forest stood all about them in the singing stillness. "Tomorrow I'll come with Uma's little brother to show him the way here. He'll be the village goatherd now. The day after tomorrow is my wedding day."

The white donkey stood still, its curly, silky beard resting against her hand.

"Nana is giving me her gold bangle," Sita said to the donkey. "I get to wear a red sari, and have henna on my feet and hands."

The donkey stood still, listening.

"There'll be sweet rice to eat at the wedding," Sita said; then she began to cry.

"Goodbye, white donkey," she said. The white donkey looked at her sidelong, and slowly, not looking back, moved away from her and walked into the darkness under the trees.

(1980)

Horse Camp

ALL THE OTHER SENIORS WERE OVER AT THE street side of the parking lot, but Sal stayed with Norah while they waited for the bus drivers. "Maybe you'll be in the creek cabin," Sal said, quiet and serious. "I had it second year. It's the best one. Number Five."

"How do they, when do you, like find out, what cabin?"

"They better remember we're in the same cabin," Ev said, sounding shrill. Norah did not look at her. She and Ev had planned for months and known for weeks that they were to be cabin-mates, but what good was that if they never found their cabin, and also Sal was not looking at Ev, only at Norah. Sal was cool, a tower of ivory. "They show you around, as soon as you get there," she said, her quiet voice speaking directly to Norah's lastnight dream of never finding the room where she had to take a test she was late for and looking among endless thatched barracks in a forest of thin black trees growing very close together like hair under a hand-lens. Norah had told no one the dream and now remembered and forgot it. "Then you have dinner, and First Campfire," Sal said. "Kimmy's going to be a counselor again. She's really neat. Listen, you tell old Meredy..."

Norah drew breath. In all the histories of Horse Camp which she had asked for and heard over and over for three years—the thunderstorm story, the horsethief story, the wonderful Stevens Mountain stories—in all of them Meredy the handler had been, Meredy said, Meredy did, Meredy knew.

"Tell him I said hi," Sal said, with a shadowy smile, looking across the parking lot at the far, insubstantial towers of downtown. Behind them the doors of the Junior Girls bus gasped open. One after another the engines of the four busses roared and spewed. Across the asphalt in the hot morning light small figures were lining up and climbing into the Junior Boys bus. High, rough, faint voices bawled. "OK, hey, have fun," Sal said. She hugged Norah and then, keeping a hand on her arm, looked down at her intently for a moment from the tower of ivory. She turned away. Norah watched her walk lightfoot and buxom across the black gap to the others of her kind who enclosed her, greeting her, "Sal! Hey, Sal!"

Ev was twitching and nickering, "Come on, Nor, come on, we'll have to sit way at the back, come on!" Side by side they pressed into the line below the gaping doorway of the bus.

In Number Five cabin four iron cots, thin-mattressed, grey-blanketed, stood strewn with bottles of insect repellent and styling mousse, T-shirts lettered UCSD and I ❤ Teddy Bears, a flashlight, an apple, a comb with hair caught in it, a paperback book open face down: *The Black Colt of Pirate Island*. Over the shingle roof huge second-growth redwoods cast deep shade, and a few feet below the porch the creek ran out into sunlight over brown stones streaming bright green weed. Behind the cabin Jim Meredith the horse-handler, a short man of fifty who had ridden as a jockey in his teens, walked along the well-beaten path, quick and a bit bowlegged. Meredith's lips were pressed firmly together. His eyes, narrow and darting, glanced from cabin to cabin, from side to side. Far through the trees high voices cried.

The Counselors know what is to be known. Red Ginger, blonde Kimmy, and beautiful black Sue: they know the vices of Pal, and how to keep Trigger from putting her head down and drinking for ten minutes from every creek. They strike the great shoulders smartly, "Aw, get over, you big lunk!" They know how to swim underwater, how to sing in harmony, how to get seconds, and when a shoe is loose. They know where they are. They know where the rest of Horse Camp is. "Home Creek runs into Little River here," Kimmy says, drawing lines in the soft dust with a redwood twig that breaks. "Senior Girls here, Senior Boys across there, Junior Birdmen about here."—"Who needs 'em?" says Sue, yawning. "Come on, who's going to help me walk the mares?"

They were all around the campfire on Quartz Meadow after the long first day of the First Overnight. The counselors were still singing, but very soft, so soft you almost couldn't hear them, lying in the sleeping bag listening to One Spot stamp and Trigger snort and the shifting at the pickets, standing in the fine, cool alpine grass listening to the soft voices and the sleepers shifting and later one coyote down the mountain singing all alone.

'Nothing wrong with you. Get up!" said Meredy, and slapped her hip. Turning her long, delicate head to him with a deprecating gaze, Philly got to her feet. She stood a moment, shuddering the reddish silk of her flank as if to dislodge flies, tested her left foreleg with caution, and then walked on, step by step. Step by step, watching, Norah went with her. Inside her body there was still a deep trembling. As she passed him, the handler just nodded. "You're all right," he meant. She was all right.

Freedom, the freedom to run, freedom is to run. Freedom is galloping. What else can it be? Only other ways to run, imitations of galloping across great highlands with the wind. Oh Philly sweet Philly my love! If Ev and Trigger couldn't keep up she'd slow down and come round in a while, after a while, over there, across the long, long field of grass, once she had learned this by heart and knew it forever, the purity, the pure joy.

"Right leg, Nor," said Meredy. And passed on to Cass and Tammy.

You have to start with the right fore. Everything else is all right. Freedom depends on this, that you start with the right fore, that long leg well balanced on its elegant pastern, that you set down that tiptoe middle-fingernail so hard and round, and spurn the dirt. Highstepping, trot past old Meredy, who always hides his smile

Shoulder to shoulder, she and Ev, in the long neat of afternoon, in a trance of light, across the home creek in the dry wild oats and cow parsley of the Long Pasture. "I was afraid before I came here," thinks Norah, incredulous, remembering childhood. She leans her head against Ev's firm and silken side. The sting of small flies awakens, the swish of long tails sends to sleep. Down by the creek in a patch of coarse grass Philly grazes and dozes. Sue comes striding by, winks wordless, beautiful as a burning coal, lazy and purposeful, bound for the shade of the willows. Is it worth getting up to go down to get your feet in the cool water? Next year Sal will be too old for a camper, but can come back as a counselor, come back here. Norah will come back a second-year camper, Sal a counselor. They will be here. This is what freedom is, what goes on, the sun in summer, the wild grass, coming back each year.

Coming back from the Long Pack Trip to Stevens Mountain weary and dirty, thirsty and in bliss, coming down from the high places, in line, Sue jogging just in front of her and Ev half asleep behind her, some sound or motion caught and turned Norah's head to look across the alpine field. On the far side under dark firs a line of horses, mounted and with packs—"Look!"

Ev snorted, Sue flicked her ears and stopped. Norah halted in line behind her, stretching her neck to see. She saw her sister going first in the distant line, the small head proudly borne. She was walking lightfoot and easy, fresh, just starting up to the high passes of the mountain. On her back a young man sat erect, his fine, fair head turned a little aside, to the forest. One hand was on his thigh, the other on the reins, guiding her. Norah called out and then broke from the line, going to Sal, calling out to her. "No, no, no, no!" she called. Behind her Ev and then Sue called to her, "Nor! Nor!"

Sal did not hear or heed. Going straight ahead, the color of ivory, distant in the clear, dry light, she stepped into the shadow of the trees. The others and their riders followed, jogging one after the other till the last was gone.

Norah had stopped in the middle of the meadow, and stood in grass in sunlight. Flies hummed.

She tossed her head, turned, and trotted back to the line. She went along it from one to the next, teasing, chivying, Kimmy yelling at her to get back in line, till Sue broke out of line to chase her and she ran, and then Ev began to run, whinnying shrill, and then Cass, and Philly, and all the rest, the whole bunch, cantering first and then running flat out, running wild, racing, heading for Horse Camp and the Long Pasture, for Meredy and the long evening standing in the fenced field, in the sweet dry grass, in the fetlock-shallow water of the home creek

(1986)

VIII

Four Cat Poems

I have a dream farm which I visit at need, to go around stocking the barns, yards, and pastures. The first livestock I bring in is usually a Jersey cow and three or four sheep—Jacobs, maybe. A donkey or two. A couple of riding horses—now the farm enlarges and grows woods, hills, long trails . . . And, if only somebody wanted to work them, you can't just have them standing around, but oh, a pair of Shires! to see forged

for the great grey drayhorse his bright and battering sandal!

Sometimes a llama. Several llamas. Rabbits. Or a whole acre, fenced carefully, of guinea pigs.

Dogs, of course. Yard dogs. Large dogs. Nothing small that yaps. Large, lean, lazy deerhounds. Have to pull ticks off long soft ears while hound looks mournful. A standard poodle, most kind and courteous being. A big red chow dog, Tao dog. But listen, you dogs, if you don't treat the cats right, you're out. Understand?

All cats are balloons. All cats are petunias. All cats are mangold-wurzels. All cats are yin enough. All cats guide me.

Tabby Lorenzo

The small cat smells of bitter rue
and autumn night. His ears are scarred.
His dark footpads are like hard flowers.
On my knee he rests entirely
trusting and entirely strange,
a messenger to all indoors
from the gardens of danger.

(1984)

Black Leonard in
Negative Space

All that surrounds the cat
is not the cat, is all
that is not the cat, is all,
is everything, except the animal
It will rejoin without a seam
when he is dead. To know
that no-space is to know
what he does not, that time
is space for love and pain.
He does not need to know it.

(1978)

A Conversation with a Silence

What kept you out so late my love?

I was running, I was running in the dark.

Dawn and raining when you came home.

The trees are clouds and roads to me.
I run the sweet dirt-darkness in the rain
and up where leafy chirping sleep-warmths
nestle their blood for me. I meet my enemies
below: the White One, the Singer.

What does your brother watch from the window?

Ghosts in the other garden.
I don't see ghosts. I go farther
along the cloud-roads
to kill where darkness branches in the rain.

(1986)

For Leonard, Darko, and Burton Watson

A black and white cat
on May grass waves his tail, suns his belly
among wallflowers.
I am reading a Chinese poet
called The Old Man Who Does As He Pleases.
The cat is aware of the writing
of swallows
on the white sky.
We are both old and doing what pleases us
in the garden. Now I am writing
and the cat
is sleeping.
Whose poem is this?

(1982)

IX

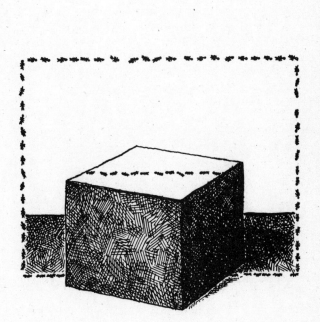

"Schrödinger's Cat" and
"The Author of the Acacia Seeds"

"Schrödinger's Cat" isn't exactly an animal story, except in this respect: The cat, which for Erwin Schrödinger was a parable-cat, a figment-cat, the amusing embodiment of a daring hypothesis, enters the story as an actual, biographico-historical cat (his name was Laurel, and his visit during the writing of the story is described exactly as [during the time that] it occurred), and so changes the thought-experiment, and its results, profoundly. So it is a story about animal presence—and absence.

So the real presence of an animal in a laboratory—that is, an animal perceived by the experimenting scientist not as an object, nor as a subject in the sense of the word 'subject of the experiment' (as in Nazi experiments in pain on human 'subjects'), but as a subject in the philosophical/grammatical sense of a sentient existence of the same order as the scientist's existence—so such presence and perception in a laboratory where experiments are performed upon animals would profoundly change the nature, and probably the results, of the experiments.

"The Author of the Acacia Seeds" records the entirely fictional results of such 'subjectivism' carried rather farther than seems probable. It grew in part out of the arguments over the experiments in language acquisition by great apes (in which, of course, if the ape is not approached as a grammatical subject, failure of the experiment is guaranteed). Some linguists deny the capacity of apes to talk in quite the same spirit in which their intellectual forebears denied the capacity of women to think. If these great men are threatened by Koko the gorilla speaking a little ASL, how would they feel reading a lab report written by the rat?

Schrödinger's Cat

AS THINGS APPEAR TO BE COMING TO SOME sort of climax, I have withdrawn to this place. It is cooler here, and nothing moves fast.

On the way here I met a married couple who were coming apart. She had pretty well gone to pieces, but he seemed, at first glance, quite hearty. While he was telling me that he had no hormones of any kind, she pulled herself together, and by supporting her head in the crook of her right knee and hopping on the toes of the right foot, approached us shouting, "Well what's *wrong* with a person trying to express themselves?" The left leg, the arms, and the trunk,which had remained lying in the heap, twitched and jerked in sympathy. "Great legs," the husband pointed out, looking at the slim ankle. "My wife has great legs."

A cat has arrived, interrupting my narrative. It is a striped yellow tom with white chest and paws. He has long whiskers and yellow eyes. I never noticed before that cats had whiskers about their eyes; is that normal? There is no way to tell. As he has gone to sleep on my knee, I shall proceed.

Where?

Nowhere, evidently. Yet the impulse to narrate remains. Many things are not worth doing, but almost anything is worth telling. In any case, I have a severe congenital case of Ethica laboris puritanica, or Adam's Disease. It is incurable except by total decapitation. I even like to dream when asleep, and to try and recall my dreams: it assures me that I haven't wasted seven or eight hours just lying there. Now here I am, lying, here. Hard at it.

Well, the couple I was telling you about finally broke up. The pieces of him trotted around bouncing and cheeping, like little chicks, but she was finally reduced to nothing but a mass of nerves: rather like fine chicken-wire, in fact, but hopelessly tangled.

So I came on, placing one foot carefully in front of the other, and grieving. This grief is with me still. I fear it is part of me, like foot or loin or eye, or may even be myself: for I seem to have no other self, nothing further, nothing that lies outside the borders of grief.

Yet I don't know what I grieve for: my wife? my husband? my children, or myself? I can't remember. Most dreams are forgotten, try as one will to remember. Yet later music strikes the note and the harmonic rings along the mandolin-strings of the mind, and we find tears in our eyes. Some note keeps playing that makes me want to cry, but what for? I am not certain.

The yellow cat, who may have belonged to the couple that broke up, is dreaming. His paws twitch now and then, and once he makes a small, suppressed remark with his mouth shut. I wonder what a cat dreams of, and to whom he was speaking just then. Cats seldom waste words. They are quiet beasts. They keep their counsel, they reflect. They reflect all day, and at night their eyes reflect. Overbred Siamese cats may be as noisy as little dogs, and then people say, "They're talking," but the noise is farther from speech than is the deep silence of the hound or the tabby. All this cat can say is meow, but maybe in his silences he will suggest to me what it is that I have lost, what I am grieving for. I have a feeling that he knows. That's why he came here. Cats look out for Number One.

It was getting awfully hot. I mean, you could touch less

and less. The stove-burners, for instance; now I know that stove-burners always used to get hot, that was their final cause, they existed in order to get hot. But they began to get hot without having been turned on. Electric units or gas rings, there they'd be when you came into the kitchen for breakfast, all four of them glaring away, the air above them shaking like clear jelly with the heatwaves. It did no good to turn them off, because they weren't on in the first place. Besides, the knobs and dials were also hot, uncomfortable to the touch.

Some people tried hard to cool them off. The favorite technique was to turn them on. It worked sometimes, but you could not count on it. Others investigated the phenomenon, tried to get at the root of it, the cause. They were probably the most frightened ones, but man is most human at his most frightened. In the face of the hot stove-burners they acted with exemplary coolness. They studied, they observed. They were like the fellow in Michelangelo's *Last Judgment*, who has clapped his hands over his face in horror as the devils drag him down to Hell—but only over one eye. the other eye is busy looking. It's all he can do, but he does it. He observes. Indeed, one wonders if Hell would exist, if he did not look at it. However, neither he, nor the people I am talking about, had enough time to do much about it. And then finally of course there were the people who did not try to do or think anything about it at all.

When the water came out of the cold-water taps hot one morning, however, even people who had blamed it all on the Democrats began to feel a more profound unease. Before long forks and pencils and wrenches were too hot to handle without gloves; and cars were really terrible. It was like opening the door of an oven going full blast, to open the door of your car. And by then, other people almost scorched your fingers off. A kiss was like a branding iron. Your child's hair flowed along your hand like fire.

Here, as I said, it is cooler; and, as a matter of fact, this animal is cool. A real cool cat. No wonder it's pleasant to pet his fur. Also he moves slowly, at least for the most part, which is all the slowness one can reasonably expect of a cat. He hasn't that frenetic quality most creatures acquired—all they did was ZAP and gone. They lacked presence. I suppose birds always tended to be that way, but even the hummingbird used to halt for a second in the very center of his metabolic frenzy, and hang, still as a hub, present, above the fuchsias—then gone again, but you knew something was there besides the blurring brightness. But it got so that even robins and pigeons, the heavy impudent birds, were a blur; and as for swallows, they cracked the sound barrier. You knew of swallows only by the small, curved sonic booms that looped about the eaves of old nouses in the evening.

Worms shot like subway trains through the dirt of gardens, among the writhing roots of roses.

You could scarcely lay a hand on children, by then: too fast to catch, too hot to hold. They grew up before your eyes.

But then, maybe that's always been true.

I was interrupted by the cat, who woke and said meow once, then jumped down from my lap and leaned against my legs diligently. This is a cat who knows how to get fed. He also knows how to jump. There was a lazy fluidity to his leap, as if gravity affected him less than it does other creatures. As a matter of fact there were some localized cases, just before I left, of the failure of gravity; but this quality in the cat's leap was something quite else. I am not yet in such a state of confusion that I can be alarmed by grace. Indeed, I found it reassuring. While I was opening a can of sardines, a person arrived.

Hearing the knock, I thought it might be the mailman. I

miss mail very much, so I hurried to the door and said, "Is it the mail?" A voice replied, "Yah!" I opened the door. He came in, almost pushing me aside in his haste. He dumped down an enormous knapsack he had been crying, straightened up, massaged his shoulders, and said, "Wow!"

"How did you get here?"

He stared at me and repeated, "How?"

At this my thoughts concerning human and animal speech recurred to me, and I decided that this was probably not a man, but a small dog. (Large dogs seldom go yah, wow, how, unless it is appropriate to do so.)

"Come on, fella," I coaxed him. "Come, come on, that's a boy, good doggie!" I opened a can of pork and beans for him at once, for he looked half starved. He ate voraciously, gulping and lapping. When it was gone he said "Wow!" several times. I was just about to scratch him behind the ears when he stiffened, his hackles bristling, and growled deep in his throat. He had noticed the cat.

The cat had noticed him some time before, without interest, and was now sitting on a copy of *The Well-Tempered Clavier* washing sardine oil off its whiskers. "Wow!" the dog, whom I had thought of calling Rover, barked.

"Wow! Do you know what that is? *That's Schrödinger's Cat!*"

"No it's not; not any more; it's my cat," I said, unreasonably offended.

"Oh, well, Schrödinger's dead, of course, but it's his cat. I've seen hundreds of picture of it. Erwin Schrödinger, the great physicist, you know. Oh, wow! To think of finding it here!"

The cat looked coldly at him for a moment, and began to wash its left shoulder with negligent energy. An almost religious expression had come into Rover's face. "It was meant," he said in a low, impressive tone. "Yah. It was *meant.* It can't be a mere coincidence. It's too improbable. Me, with the box; you, with the cat; to meet—here—now." He looked up at me, his eyes shining with happy fervor. "Isn't it wonderful?" he said. "I'll get the box set up right away." And he started to tear open his huge knapsack.

While the cat washed its front paws, Rover unpacked. While the cat washed its tail and belly, regions hard to reach gracefully, Rover put together what he had unpacked, a complex task. When he and the cat finished their operations simultaneously and looked at me, I was impressed. They had come out even, to the very second. Indeed it seemed that something more than chance was involved. I hoped it was not myself.

"What's that?" I asked, pointing to a protuberance on the outside of the box. I did not ask what the box was as it was quite clearly a box.

"The gun," Rover said with excited pride.

"The gun?"

"To shoot the cat."

"To shoot the cat?"

"Or to *not shoot* the cat. Depending on the photon."

"The photon?"

"Yah! It's Schrödinger's great Gedankenexperiment. You see, there's a little emitter here. At Zero Time, five seconds after the lid of the box is closed, it will emit one photon. The photon will strike a half-silvered mirror. The quantum mechanical probability of the photon passing through the mirror is exactly one-half, isn't it? So! If the photon passes through, the trigger will be activated and the gun will fire. If the photon is deflected, the trigger will not be activated and the gun will not fire. Now, you put the cat in. The cat is in the box. You close the lid. You go away! You stay away! What happens?" Rover's eyes were bright.

"The cat gets hungry?"

"The cat gets shot—or not shot," he said, seizing my arm,

though not, fortunately, in his teeth. "But the gun is silent, perfectly silent. The box is soundproof. There is no way to know whether or not the cat has been shot, until you lift the lid of the box. There is NO way! Do you see how central this is to the whole of quantum theory? Before Zero Time the whole system, on the quantum level or on our level, is nice and simple. But after Zero Time the whole system can be represented only by a linear combination of two waves. We cannot predict the behavior of the photon, and thus, once it has behaved, we cannot predict the state of the system it has determined. We cannot predict it! God plays dice with the world! So it is beautifully demonstrated that if you desire certainty, any certainty, you must create it yourself!"

"How?"

"By lifting the lid of the box, of course," Rover said, looking at me with sudden disappointment, perhaps a touch of suspicion, like a Baptist who finds he has been talking church matters not to another Baptist as he thought, but a Methodist, or even, God forbid, an Episcopalian. "To find out whether the cat is dead or not."

"Do you mean," I said carefully, "that until you lift the lid of the box, the cat has neither been shot nor not been shot?"

"Yah!" Rover said, radiant with relief, welcoming me back to the fold. "Or maybe, you know, both."

"But why does opening the box and looking reduce the system back to one probability, either live cat or dead cat? Why don't we get included in the system when we lift the lid of the box?"

There was a pause. "How?" Rover barked, distrustfully.

"Well, we would involve ourselves in the system, you see, the superposition of two waves. There's no reason why it should only exist *inside* an open box, is there? so when we came to look, there we would be, you and I, both looking at a live cat, and both looking at a dead cat. You see?"

A dark cloud lowered on Rover's eyes and brow. He barked twice in a subdued, harsh voice, and walked away. With his back turned to me he said in a firm, sad tone, "You must not complicate the issue. It is complicated enough."

"Are you sure?"

He nodded. Turning, he spoke pleadingly. "Listen. It's all we have—the box. Truly it is. The box. And the cat. And they're here. The box, the cat, at last. Put the cat in the box. Will you? Will you let me put the cat in the box?"

"No," I said, shocked.

"Please. Please. Just for a minute. Just for half a minute! Please let me put the cat in the box!"

"Why?"

"I can't stand this terrible uncertainty," he said, and burst into tears.

I stood some while indecisive. Though I felt sorry for the poor son of a bitch, I was about to tell him, gently, No; when a curious thing happened. The cat walked over to the box, sniffed around it, lifted his tail and sprayed a corner to mark his territory, and then lightly, with that marvelous fluid ease, leapt into it. His yellow tail just flicked the edge of the lid as he jumped, and it closed, falling into place with a soft, decisive click.

"The cat is in the box," I said.

"The cat is in the box," Rover repeated in a whisper, falling to his knees. "Oh, wow. Oh, wow. Oh, wow."

There was silence then: deep silence. We both gazed, I afoot, Rover kneeling, at the box. No sound. Nothing happened. Nothing would happen. Nothing would ever happen, until we lifted the lid of the box.

"Like Pandora," I said in a weak whisper. I could not quite recall Pandora's legend. She had let all the plagues and evils out of the box, of course, but there had been something else, too. After all the devils were let loose, something quite different, quite unexpected, had been left. What had it been? Hope? A dead cat? I could not remember.

Impatience welled up in me. I turned on Rover, glaring. He returned the look with expressive brown eyes. You can't tell me dogs haven't got souls.

"Just exactly what are you trying to prove?" I demanded.

"That the cat will be dead, or not dead," he murmured submissively. "Certainty. All I want is certainty. To know for *sure* that God *does* play dice with the world!"

I looked at him for a while with fascinated incredulity. "Whether he does, or doesn't," I said, "do you think he's going to leave you a note about it in the box?" I went to the box, and with a rather dramatic gesture, flung the lid back. Rover staggered up from his knees, gasping, to look. The cat was, of course, not there.

Rover neither barked, nor fainted, nor cursed, nor wept. He really took it very well.

"Where is the cat?" he asked at last.

"Where is the box?"

"Here."

"Where's here?"

"Here is now."

"We used to think so," I said, "but really we could use larger boxes."

He gazed about him in mute bewilderment, and did not flinch even when the roof of the house was lifted off just like the lid of a box, letting in the unconscionable, inordinate light of the stars. He had just time to breathe, "Oh, wow!"

I have identified the note that keeps sounding. I checked it on the mandolin before the glue melted. It is the note A, the one that drove the composer Schumann mad. It is a beautiful, clear tone, much clearer now that the stars are visible. I shall miss the cat. I wonder if he found what it was we lost.

(1974)

"The Author of the Acacia Seeds" and Other Extracts from the *Journal of the Association of Therolinguistics*

MS. FOUND IN AN ANT-HILL

The messages were found written in touch-gland exudation on degerminated acacia seeds laid in rows at the end of a narrow, erratic tunnel leading off from one of the deeper levels of the colony. It was the orderly arrangement of the seeds that first drew the investigator's attention. The messages are fragmentary, and the translation approximate and highly interpretative; but the text seems worthy of interest if only for its striking lack of resemblance to any other Ant texts known to us.

> SEEDS 1-13
> [I will] not touch feelers. [I will] not stroke. [I will] spend on dry seeds [my] soul's sweetness. It may be found when [I am] dead. Touch this dry wood! [I] call! [I am] here!

Alternatively, this passage may be read:

> [Do] not touch feelers. [Do] not stroke. Spend on dry seeds [your] soul's sweetness. [Others] may find it when [you are] dead. Touch this dry wood! Call: [I am] here!

No known dialect of Ant employs any verbal person except the third person singular and plural, and the first person plural. In this text, only the root-forms of the verbs are used; so there is no way to decide whether the passage was intended to be an autobiography or a manifesto.

SEEDS 14-22
Long are the tunnels. Longer is the untunneled. No
tunnel reaches the end of the untunneled. The untunneled goes on farther than we can go in ten days
[*i.e.*, forever]. Praise!

The mark translated "Praise!" is half of the customary salutation "Praise the Queen!" or "Long live the Queen!" or "Huzza for the Queen!"—but the word/mark signifying "Queen" has been omitted.

SEEDS 23-29
As the ant among foreign-enemy ants is killed, so the
ant without ants dies, but being without ants is as
sweet as honeydew.

An ant intruding in a colony not its own is usually killed. Isolated from other ants it invariably dies within a day or so. The difficulty in this passage is the word/mark "without ants," which we take to mean "alone"—a concept for which no word/mark exists in Ant.

SEEDS 30-31
Eat the eggs! Up with the Queen!

There has already been considerable dispute over the interpretation of the phrase on Seed 31. It is an important question, since all the preceding seeds can be fully understood only in the light cast by this ultimate exhortation. Dr. Rosbone ingeniously argues that the author, a wingless neuter-female worker, yearns hopelessly to be a winged male, and to found a new colony, flying upward in the nuptial flight with a new Queen. Though the text certainly permits such a reading, our conviction is that nothing in the text *supports* it—least of all the text of the immediately preceding seed, No. 30: "Eat the eggs!" This reading, though shocking, is beyond disputation.

We venture to suggest that the confusion over Seed 31 may result from an ethnocentric interpretation of the word "up." To us, "up" is a "good" direction. Not so, or not necessarily so, to an ant. "Up" is where the food comes from, to be sure; but "down" is where security, peace, and home are to be found. "Up" is the scorching sun; the freezing night; no shelter in the beloved tunnels; exile; death. Therefore we suggest that this strange author, in the solitude of her lonely tunnel, sought with what means she had to express the ultimate blasphemy conceivable to an ant, and that the correct reading of Seeds 30-31, in human terms is:

Eat the eggs! Down with the Queen!

The desicated body of a small worker was found beside Seed 31 when the manuscript was discovered. The head had been severed from the thorax, probably by the jaws of a soldier of the colony. The seeds, carefully arranged in a pattern resembling a musical stave, had not been disturbed. (Ants of the soldier caste are illiterate; thus the soldier was presumably not interested in the collection of useless seeds from which the edible germs had been removed.) No living ants were left in the colony, which was destroyed in a war with a neighboring ant-hill at some time subsequent to the death of the Author of the Acadia Seeds.

—G. D'Arbay, T.R. Bardol

ANNOUNCEMENT OF AN EXPEDITION

The extreme difficulty of reading Penguin has been very much lessened by the use of the underwater motion picture camera. On film it is at least possible to repeat, and to slow down, the fluid sequences of the script, to the point where, by constant repetition and patient study, many elements of this most elegant and lively literature may be grasped, though the nuances, and perhaps the essence, must forever elude us.

It was Professor Duby who, by pointing out the remote affiliation of the script with Low Graylag, made possible the first, tentative glossary of Penguin. The analogies with Dolphin which had been employed up to that time never proved very useful, and were often quite misleading.

Indeed it seemed strange that a script written almost entirely in wings, neck, and air, should prove the key to the poetry of short-necked, flipper-winged water-writers. But we should not have found it so strange if we had kept in mind the fact that penguins are, despite all evidence to the contrary, birds.

Because their script resembles Dolphin in *form*, we should never have assumed that it must resemble Dolphin in *content*. And indeed it does not. There is, of course, the same extraordinary wit and the flashes of crazy humor, the inventiveness, and the inimitable grace. In all the thousands of literatures of the Fish stock, only a few show any humor at all, and that usually of a rather simple, primitive sort; and the superb gracefulness of Shark or Tarpon is utterly different from the joyous vigor of all Cetacean scripts. The joy, the vigor, and the humor are all shared by Penguin authors; and, indeed, by many of the finer Seal *auteurs*. The temperature of the blood is a bond. But the construction of the brain, and of the womb, makes a barrier! Dolphins do not lay eggs. A world of difference lies in that simple fact.

Only when Professor Duby reminded us that penguins are birds, that they do not swim but *fly in water*, only then could the therolinguist begin to approach the sea-literature of the penguin with understanding; only then could the miles of recordings already on film be re-studied and, finally, appreciated.

But the difficulty of translation is still with us.

A satisfying degree of progress has already been made in Adelie. The difficulties of recording a group kinetic performance in a stormy ocean as thick as pea-soup with plankton at a temperature of 31°F are considerable; but the perseverance of the Ross Ice Barrier Literary Circle has been fully rewarded with such passages as "Under the Iceberg," from the *Autumn Song*—a passage now world famous in the rendition of Anna Serebryakova of the Leningrad Ballet. No verbal rendering can approach the felicity of Miss Serebryakova's version. For, quite simply, there is no way to reproduce in writing the all-important *multiplicity* of the original text, so beautifully rendered by the full chorus of the Leningrad Ballet company. Indeed, what we call "translations" from the Adelie—or from any group kinetic text—are, to put it bluntly, mere notes—libretto without the opera. The ballet version is the true translation. Nothing in words can be complete.

I therefore suggest, though the suggestion may well be greeted with frowns of anger or with hoots of laughter, that for the therolinguist—as opposed to the artist and the amateur—the kinetic sea-writings of Penguin are the *least* promising field of study: and, further, that Adelie, for all its charm and relative simplicity, is a less promising field of study than is Emperor.

Emperor!—I anticipate my colleagues' response to this suggestion. Emperor! The most difficult, the most remote, of all the dialects of Penguin! The language of which Professor Duby himself remarked, "The literature of the emperor penguin is as forbidding, as inaccessible, as the frozen heart of Anartica itself. Its beauties may be unearthly, but they are not for us."

Maybe. I do not underestimate the difficulties: not least of which is the Imperial temperament, so much more reserved and aloof than that of any other penguin. But, paradoxically, it is just in this reserve that I place my hope. The emperor is not a solitary, but a social bird, and while on land for the breeding season dwells in colonies, as does the adelie; but these colonies are very much smaller and very much quieter than those of the adelie. The bonds between the members of an emperor colony are rather personal than social. The emperor is an individualist. Therefore I think it almost certain that the literature of the emperor will prove to be composed by single authors, instead of chorally; and therefore it will be translatable into human speech. It will be a kinetic literature, but how different from the spatially extensive, rapid, multiplex choruses of sea-writing! Close analysis, and genuine transcription, will at last be possible.

What! say my critics—Should we pack up and go to Cape Crozier, to the dark, to the blizzards, to the –60° cold, in the mere hope of recording the problematic poetry of a few strange birds who sit there, in the mid-winter dark, in the blizzards, in the –60° cold, on the eternal ice, with an egg on their feet?

And my reply is, Yes. For, like Professor Duby, my instinct tells me that the beauty of that poetry is as unearthly as anything we shall ever find on earth.

To those of my colleagues in whom the spirit of scientific curiosity and aesthetic risk is strong, I say, imagine it: the ice, the scouring snow, the darkness, the ceaseless whine and scream of wind. In that black desolation a little band of poets crouches. They are starving; they will not eat for weeks. On the feet of each one, under the warm belly-feathers, rests one large egg, thus preserved from the mortal touch of the ice. The poets cannot hear each other; they cannot see each other. They can only feel the other's *warmth.* That is their poetry, that is their art. Like all kinetic literatures, it is silent; unlike other kinetic literatures, it is all but immobile, ineffably subtle. The ruffling of a feather; the shifting of a wing; the touch, the slight, faint, warm touch of the one beside you. In unutterable, miserable, black solitude, the affirmation. In absence, presence. In death, life.

I have obtained a sizable grant from UNESCO and have stocked an expedition. There are still four places open. We leave for Antarctica on Thursday. If anyone wants to come along, welcome!

—D. Petri

EDITORIAL BY THE PRESIDENT OF THE THEROLINGUISTICS ASSOCIATION

What is Language?

This question, central to the science of therolinguists, has been answered—heuristically—by the very existence of the science. Language is communication. That is the axiom on which all our theory and research rest, and from which all our discoveries derive; and the success of the discoveries testifies to the validity of the axiom. But to the related, yet not identical question, What is Art? we have not yet given a satisfactory answer.

Tolstoy, in the book whose title is that very question, answered it firmly and clearly: Art, too, is communication. This answer has, I believe, been accepted without examination or criticism by therolinguistics. For example: Why do therolinguists study only animals?

Why, because plants do not communicate.

Plants do not communicate; that is a fact. Therefore plants have no language; very well; that follows from our basic axiom. Therefore, also, plants have no art. But stay!

That does *not* follow from the basic axiom, but only from the unexamined Tolstoyan corollary.

What if art is not communicative?

Or, what if some art is communicative, and some art is not?

Ourselves animals, active, predators, we look (naturally enough) for an active, predatory, communicative art; and when we find it, we recognize it. The development of this power of recognition and the skills of appreciation is a recent and glorious achievement.

But I submit that, for all the tremendous advances made by therolinguistics during the last decades, we are only at the beginning of our age of discovery. We must not become slaves to our own axioms. We have not yet lifted our eyes to the vaster horizons before us. We have not faced the almost terrifying challenge of the Plant.

If a non-communicative, vegetative art exists, we must re-think the very elements of our science, and learn a whole new set of techniques.

For it is simply not possible to bring the critical and technical skills appropriate to the study of Weasel murder-mysteries, or Batrachian erotica, or the tunnel-sagas of the earthworm, to bear on the art of the redwood or the zucchini.

This is proved conclusively by the failure—a noble failure—of the efforts of Dr. Srivas, in Calcutta, using time-lapse photography, to produce a lexicon of Sunflower. His attempt was daring, but doomed to failure. For his approach was kinetic—a method appropriate to the *communicative* arts of the tortoise, the oyster, and the sloth. He saw the extreme slowness of the kinesis of plants, and only that, as the problem to be solved.

But the problem was far greater. The art he sought, if it exists, is a non-communicative art: and probably a non-kinetic one. It is possible that Time, the essential element, matrix, and measure of all known animal art, does not enter into vegetable art at all. The plants may use the meter of eternity. We do not know.

We do not know. All we can guess is that the putative Art of the Plant is *entirely different* from the Art of the Animal. What it is, we cannot say; we have not yet discovered it. Yet I predict with some certainty that it exists, and that when it is found it will prove to be, not an action, but a reaction: not a communication, but a reception. It will be exactly the opposite of the art we know and recognize. It will be the first *passive* art known to us. Can we in fact know it? Can we ever understand it?

It will be immensely difficult. That is clear. But we should not despair. Remember that so late as the mid-twentieth century, most scientists, and many artists, did not believe that even Dolphin would ever be comprehensible to the human brain—or worth comprehending! Let another century pass, and we may seem equally laughable. "Do you realize," the phytolinguist will say to the aesthetic critic, "that they couldn't even read Eggplant?" And they will smile at our ignorance, as they pick up their rucksacks and hike on up to read the newly deciphered lyrics of the lichen on the north face of Pike's Peak.

And with them, or after them, may there not come that even bolder adventurer—the first geolinguist, who, ignoring the delicate, transient lyrics of the lichen, will read beneath it the still less communicative, still more passive, wholly atemporal, cold, volcanic poetry of the rocks: each one a word spoken, how long ago, by the earth itself, in the immense solitude, the immenser community, of space.

(1974)

X

and the way I remember it, it was a mountain lion. And the way I remember May telling it is sitting on the edge of the irrigation tank we used to swim in, cement rough as a lava flow and hot in the sun, the long cracks tarred over. She was an old lady then with a long Irish upper lip, kind and wary and balky. She liked to come sit and talk with my mother while I swam; she didn't have all that many people to talk to. She always had chickens, in the chickenhouse very near the back door of the farmhouse, so the whole place smelled pretty strong of chickens, and as long as she could she kept a cow or two down in the old barn by the creek. The first of May's cows I remember was Pearl, a big, handsome Holstein who gave fourteen or twenty-four or forty gallons or quarts of milk at a milking, whichever is right for a prize milker. Pearl was beautiful in my eyes when I was four or five years old; I loved and admired her. I remember how excited I was, how I reached upward to them, when Pearl or the workhorse Prince, for whom my love amounted to worship, would put an immense and sensitive muzzle through the three-strand fence to whisk a cornhusk from my fearful hand; and then the munching; and the sweet breath and the big nose would be at the barbed wire again: the offering is acceptable.... After Pearl there was Rosie, a purebred Jersey. May got her either cheap or free because she was a runt calf, so tiny that May brought her home on her lap in the back of the car, like a fawn. And Rosie always looked like she had some deer in her. She was a lovely, clever little cow and even more willful than old May. She often chose not to come in to be milked. We would hear May calling and then see her trudging across our lower pasture with the bucket, going to find Rosie wherever Rosie had decided to be milked today on the wild hills she had to roam in, a hundred acres of our and Old Jim's land. Then May had a fox terrier named Pinky, who yipped and nipped and turned me against fox terriers for life, but he was long gone when the mountain lion came; and the black cats who lived in the barn kept discreetly out of the story. As a matter of fact now I think of it the chickens weren't in it either. It might have been quite different if they had been. May had quit keeping chickens after old Mrs. Walter died. It was just her all alone there, and Rosie and the cats down in the barn, and nobody else within sight or sound of the old farm. We were in our house up the hill only in the summer, and Jim lived in town, those years. What time of year it was I don't know, but I imagine the grass still green or just turning gold. And May was in the house, in the kitchen, where she lived entirely unless she was asleep or outdoors, when she heard this noise.

Now you need May herself, sitting skinny on the edge of the irrigation tank, seventy or eighty or ninety years old, nobody knew how old May was and she had made sure they couldn't find out, opening her pleated lips and letting out this noise—a huge, awful yowl, starting soft with a nasal hum and rising slowly into a snarling gargle that sank away into a sobbing purr.... It got better every time she told the story.

"It was some meow," she said.

So she went to the kitchen door, opened it, and looked out. Then she shut the kitchen door and went to the kitchen window to look out, because there was a mountain lion under the fig tree.

Puma, cougar, catamount; *Felis concolor*; the shy, secret, shadowy lion of the New World, four or five feet long plus a yard of black-tipped tail, weighs about what a woman weighs, lives where the deer live from Canada to Chile, but always shyer, always fewer; the color of dry leaves, dry grass.

There were plenty of deer in the Valley in the forties, but no mountain lion had been seen for decades anywhere near where people lived. Maybe way back up in the canyons; but Jim, who hunted, and knew every deer-trail in the hills, had never seen a lion. Nobody had, except May, now, alone in her kitchen.

"I thought maybe it was sick," she told us. "It wasn't acting right. I don't think a lion would walk right into the yard like that if it was feeling well. If I'd still had the chickens it'd be a different story maybe! But it just walked around some, and then it lay down there," and she points between the fig tree and the decrepit garage. "And then after a while it kind of meowed again, and got up and come into the shade right there." The fig tree, planted when the house was built, about the time May was born, makes a great, green, sweet-smelling shade. "It just laid there looking around. It wasn't well," says May.

She had lived with and looked after animals all her life; she had also earned her living for years as a nurse.

"Well, I didn't know exactly what to do for it. So I put out some water for it. It didn't even get up when I come out the door. I put the water down there, not so close to it that we'd scare each other, see, and it kept watching me, but it didn't move. After I went back in it did get up and tried to drink some water. Then it made that kind of meowowow. I do believe it come here because it was looking for help. Or just for company, maybe."

The afternoon went on, May in the kitchen, the lion under the fig tree.

But down in the barnyard by the creek was Rosie the cow. Fortunately the gate was shut, so she could not come wandering up to the house and meet the lion; but she would be needing to be milked, come six or seven o'clock, and that got to worrying May. She also worried how long a sick mountain lion might hang around, keeping her shut in the house. May didn't like being shut in.

"I went out a time or two, and went shoo!"

Eyes shining amidst fine wrinkles, she flaps her thin arms at the lion. "Shoo! Go on home now!"

But the silent wild creature watches her with yellow eyes and does not stir.

"So when I was talking to Miss Macy on the telephone, she said it might have rabies, and I ought to call the sheriff. I was uneasy then. So finally I did that, and they come out, those county police, you know. Two carloads."

Her voice is dry and quiet.

"I guess there was nothing else they knew how to do. So they shot it."

She looks off across the field Old Jim, her brother, used to plow with Prince the horse and irrigate with the water from this tank. Now wild oats and blackberry grow there. In another thirty years it will be a rich man's vineyard, a tax write-off.

"He was seven feet long, all stretched out, before they took him off. And so thin! They all said, 'Well, Aunt May, I guess you were scared there! I guess you were some scared!' But I wasn't. I didn't want him shot. But I didn't know what to do for him. And I did need to get to Rosie."

I have told this true story which May gave to us as truly as I could, and now I want to tell it as fiction, yet without taking it from her: rather to give it back to her, if I can do so. It is a tiny part of the history of the Valley, and I want to make it part of the Valley outside history. Now the field that the poor man plowed and the rich man harvested lies on the edge of a little town, houses and workshops of timber and fieldstone standing among almond, oak, and eucalyptus trees; and now May is an old woman with a name that means the month of May: Rains End. An old woman with a long, wrinkled-pleated upper lip, she is living alone for the summer in her summer place, a meadow a mile or so up in the hills above the little town. Sinshan. She took her cow Rose with her, and since Rose tends to wander she keeps her on a long tether down by the tiny creek, and moves her into fresh grass now and then. The summerhouse is what they call a nine-pole house, a mere frame of poles stuck in the ground—one of them is a live digger-pine sapling—with stick and matting walls, and mat roof and floors. It doesn't rain in the dry season, and the roof is just for shade. But the house and its little front yard where Rains End has her camp stove and clay oven and matting loom are well shaded by a fig tree that was planted there a hundred years or so ago by her grandmother.

Rains End herself has no grandchildren; she never bore a child, and her one or two marriages were brief and very long ago. She has a nephew and two grandnieces, and feels herself an aunt to all children, even when they are afraid of her and rude to her because she has got so ugly with old age, smelling as musty as a chickenhouse. She considers it natural for children to shrink away from somebody part way dead, and knows that when they're a little older and have got used to her they'll ask her for stories. She was for sixty years a member of the Doctors Lodge, and though she doesn't do curing any more people still ask her to help with nursing sick children, and the children come to long for the kind, authoritative touch of her hands when she bathes them to bring a fever down, or changes a dressing, or combs out bed-tangled hair with witch hazel and great patience.

So Rains End was just waking up from an early afternoon nap in the heat of the day, under the matting roof, when she heard a noise, a huge, awful yowl that started soft with a nasal hum and rose slowly into a snarling gargle that sank away into a sobbing purr.... And she got up and looked out from the open side of the house of sticks and matting, and saw a mountain lion under the fig tree. She looked at him from her house; he looked at her from his.

And this part of the story is much the same: the old woman; the lion; and, down by the creek, the cow.

It was hot. Crickets sang shrill in the yellow grass on all the hills and canyons, in all the chaparral. Rains End filled a bowl with water from an unglazed jug and came slowly out of the house. Halfway between the house and the lion she set the bowl down on the dirt. She turned and went back to the house.

The lion got up after a while and came and sniffed at the water. He lay down again with a soft, querulous groan, almost like a sick child, and looked at Rains End with the yellow eyes that saw her in a different way than she had ever been seen before.

She sat on the matting in the shade of the open part of her house and did some mending. When she looked up at the lion she sang under her breath, tunelessly; she wanted to remember the Puma Dance Song but could only remember bits of it, so she made a song for the occasion:

> You are there, lion.
> You are there, lion. . . .

As the afternoon wore on she began to worry about going down to milk Rose. Unmilked, the cow would start tugging at her tether and making a commotion. That was likely to upset the lion. He lay so close to the house now that if she came out that too might upset him, and she did not want to frighten him or to become frightened of him. He had evidently come for some reason, and it behoved her to find out what the reason was. Probably he was sick; his coming so close to a human person was strange, and people who behave strangely are usually sick or in some kind of pain. Sometimes, though, they are spiritually moved to act strangely. The lion might be a messenger, or might have some message of his own for her or her townspeople. She was more used to seeing birds as messengers; the four-footed people go about their own business. But the lion, dweller in the Seventh House, comes from the place dreams come from. Maybe she did not understand. Maybe someone else would understand. She could go over and tell Valiant and her family, whose summerhouse was in Gahheya meadow, farther up the creek; or she could go over to Buck's, on Baldy Knoll. But there were four or five adolescents there, and one of them might come and shoot the lion, to boast that he'd saved old Rains End from getting clawed to bits and eaten.

Moooooo! said Rose, down by the creek, reproachfully.

The sun was still above the southwest ridge, but the branches of pines were across it and the heavy heat was out of it, and shadows were welling up in the low fields of wild oats and blackberry.

Moooooo! said Rose again, louder.

The lion lifted up his square, heavy head, the color of dry wild oats, and gazed down across the pastures. Rains End knew from that weary movement that he was very ill. He had come for company in dying, that was all.

"I'll come back, lion," Rains End sang tunelessly. "Lie still. Be quiet. I'll come back soon." Moving softly and easily, as she would move in a room with a sick child, she got her milking pail and stool, slung the stool on her back with a woven strap so as to leave a hand free, and came out of the house. The lion watched her at first very tense, the yellow eyes firing up for a moment, but then put his head down again with that little grudging, groaning sound. "I'll come back, lion," Rains End said. She went down to the creekside and milked a nervous and indignant cow. Rose could smell lion, and demanded in several ways, all eloquent, just what Rains End intended to *do*? Rains End ignored her questions and sang milking songs to her: "Su bonny, su bonny, be still my grand cow ..." Once she had to slap her hard on the hip. "Quit that, you old fool! Get over! I am *not* going to untie you and have you walking into trouble! I won't let him come down this way."

She did not say how she planned to stop him.

She retethered Rose where she could stand down in the creek if she liked. When she came back up the rise with the pail of milk in hand, the lion had not moved. The sun was down, the air above the ridges turning clear gold. The yellow eyes watched her, no light in them. She came to pour milk into the lion's bowl. As she did so, he all at once half rose up. Rains End started, and spilled some of the milk she was pouring. "Shoo! Stop that!" she whispered fiercely, waving her skinny arm at the lion. "Lie down now! I'm afraid of you when you get up, can't you see that, stupid? Lie down now, lion. There you are. Here I am. It's all right. You know what you're doing." Talking softly as she went, she returned to her house of stick and matting. There she sat down as before, in the open porch, on the grass mats.

The mountain lion made the grumbling sound, ending with a long sigh, and let his head sink back down on his paws.

Rains End got some cornbread and a tomato from the pantry box while there was still daylight left to see by, and ate slowly and neatly. She did not offer the lion food. He had not touched the milk, and she thought he would eat no more in the House of Earth.

From time to time as the quiet evening darkened and stars gathered thicker overhead she sang to the lion. She sang the five songs of *Going Westward to the Sunrise*, which are sung to human beings dying. She did not know if it was proper and appropriate to sing these songs to a dying mountain lion, but she did not know his songs.

Twice he also sang: once a quavering moan, like a housecat challenging another tom to battle, and once a long, sighing purr.

Before the Scorpion had swung clear of Sinshan Mountain, Rains End had pulled her heavy shawl around herself in case the fog came in, and had gone sound asleep in the porch of her house.

She woke with the grey light before sunrise. The lion was a motionless shadow, a little farther from the trunk of the fig tree than he had been the night before. As the light grew, she saw that he had stretched himself out full length. She knew he had finished his dying, and sang the fifth song, the last song, in a whisper, for him:

> The doors of the Four Houses
> are open.
> Surely they are open.

Near sunrise she went to milk Rose, and to wash in the creek. When she came back up to the house she went closer to the lion, though not so close as to crowd him, and stood for a long time looking at him stretched out in the long, tawny, delicate light. "As thin as I am!" she said to Valiant, when she went up to Gahheya later in the morning to tell the story and to ask help carrying the body of the lion off where the buzzards and coyotes could clean it.

It's still your story, Aunt May; it was your lion. He came to you. He brought his death to you, a gift; but the men with the guns won't take gifts, they think they own death already. And so they took from you the honor he did you, and you felt that loss. I wanted to restore it. But you don't need it. You followed the lion where he went, years ago now.

(1983–87)

XI

Rilke's "Eighth Duino Elegy" and
"She Unnames Them"

I learned most of my German from Mark Twain. My translation of Rilke's poem was achieved by chewing up and digesting other translations—C.F. McIntyre's still seems the truest to me—and then using a German dictionary and a lot of nerve. The "Elegy" is the poem about animals that I have loved the longest and learned the most from.

It is followed by the story that had to come last in this book because it states (equivocally, of course) whose side (so long as sides must be taken) I am on and what the consequences (maybe) are.

The Eighth Elegy
(From "The Duino Elegies" of Rainer Maria Rilke)

With all its gaze the animal
sees openness. Only our eyes are
as if reversed, set like traps
all around its free forthgoing.
What is outside, we know from the face
of the animal only; for we turn even the
     youngest child
around and force it to see all forms
backwards, not the openness
so deep in the beast's gaze. Free from death.

Only we see that. The free animal
has its dying always behind it
and God in front of it, and its way
is the eternal way, as the spring flowing.
Never, not for a moment, do we have
pure space before us, where the flowers
endlessly open. Always it's world
and never nowhere-nothing-not,
that pure unoverseen we breathe
and know without desiring forever. So a child,
losing itself in that silence, has to be
jolted back. Or one dies, and *is*.
For close to death we don't see death,
but stare outward, maybe with the beast's great gaze.
And lovers, if it weren't for the other
getting in the way, come very close to it, amazed,
as if it had been left open by mistake,
behind the beloved—but nobody
gets all the way, and it's all world again.
Facing Creation forever, all we see
in it is a mirror-image of the free
in our own dark shadow. Or an animal,
a dumb beast, stares right through us, peaceably.
This is called Destiny: being face to face,
and never anything but face to face.

Were this consciousness of ours shared by
the beast, that in its certainty approaches us
in a different direction, it would take us
with it on its way. But its being is
to it unending, uncontained, no glimpse
of its condition, pure, as is its gaze.
And where we see the Future, it sees all,
and itself in all, and healed forever.

Yet in the warm, watching animal
is the care and weight of a great sadness.
For it bears always, as we bear,
and are borne down by, memory.
As if not long ago all we yearn for
had been closer to us, truer, and the bond
endlessly tender. Here all is distance,
there it was breathing. After the first home,
the second is duplicitous, drafty.
O happiness of tiny creatures
that stay forever in the womb that bears them!
O fly's joy, buzzing still *within*,
even on its mating-day! For womb is all.
And look at the half-certainty of birds,
that from the start know almost both,
like a soul of the Etruscans
in the body shut inside the tomb,
its own resting figure as the lid.
And how distressed the womb-born are
when they must fly! As if scared
by themselves, they jerk across the air, as a crack
goes through a cup: so the bat's track
through the porcelain of twilight.

And we, onlookers, always, everywhere,
our face turned to it all and never from!
It overfills us. We control it. It breaks down.
We re-control it, and break down ourselves.
Who turned us round like this, so that
no matter what we do, we have the air
of somebody departing? As a traveller
on the last hill, for the last time seeing
all the home valley, turns, and stands, and lingers—
so we live forever taking leave.

She Unnames Them

MOST OF THEM ACCEPTED NAMELESSNESS
with the perfect indifference with which they had so long
accepted and ignored their names. Whales and dolphins,
seals and sea otters consented with particular grace and
alacrity, sliding into anonymity as into their element. A
faction of yaks, however, protested. They said that "yak"
sounded right, and that almost everyone who knew they
existed called them that. Unlike the ubiquitous creatures
such as rats or fleas who had been called by hundreds or
thousands of different names since Babel, the yaks could
truly say, they said, that they had *a name*. They discussed
the matter all summer. The councils of the elderly females
finally agreed that though the name might be useful to
others, it was so redundant from the yak point of view that
they never spoke it themselves, and hence might as well
dispense with it. After they presented the argument in this
light to their bulls, a full consensus was delayed only by the
onset of severe early blizzards. Soon after the beginning of
the thaw their agreement was reached and the designation
"yak" was returned to the donor.

Among the domestic animals, few horses had cared what
anybody called them since the failure of Dean Swift's
attempt to name them from their own vocabulary. Cattle,
sheep, swine, asses, mules, and goats, along with chickens,
geese, and turkeys, all agreed enthusiastically to give their
names back to the people to whom—as they put it—they
belonged.

A couple of problems did come up with pets. The cats of
course steadfastly denied ever having had any name other
than those self-given, unspoken, effanineffably personal

names which, as the poet named Eliot said, they spend long hours daily contemplating—though none of the contemplators has ever admitted that what they contemplate is in fact their name, and some onlookers have wondered if the object of that meditative gaze might not in fact be the Perfect, or Platonic, Mouse. In any case it is a moot point now. It was with the dogs, and with some parrots, lovebirds, ravens, and mynahs that the trouble arose. These verbally talented individuals insisted that their names were important to them, and flatly refused to part with them. But as soon as they understood that the issue was precisely one of individual choice, and that anybody who wanted to be called Rover, or Froufrou, or Polly, or even Birdie in the personal sense, was perfectly free to do so, not one of them had the least objection to parting with the lower case (or, as regards German creatures, uppercase) generic appellations poodle, parrot, dog, or bird, and all the Linnaean qualifiers that had trailed along behind them for two hundred years like tin cans tied to a tail.

The insects parted with their names in vast clouds and swarms of ephemeral syllables buzzing and stinging and humming and flitting and crawling and tunneling away.

As for the fish of the sea, their names dispersed from them in silence throughout the oceans like faint, dark blurs of cuttlefish ink, and drifted off on the currents without a trace.

None were left now to unname, and yet how close I felt to them when I saw one of them swim or fly or trot or crawl across my way or over my skin, or stalk me in the night, or go along beside me for a while in the day. They seemed far closer than when their names had stood between myself and them like a clear barrier: so close that my fear of them and their fear of me became one same fear. And the attraction that many of us felt, the desire to smell one another's smells, feel or rub or caress one another's scales or skin or feathers or fur, taste one another's blood or flesh, keep one another warm,—that attraction was now all one with the fear, and the hunter could not be told from the hunted, nor the eater from the food.

This was more or less the effect I had been after. It was somewhat more powerful than I had anticipated, but I could not now, in all conscience, make an exception for myself. I resolutely put anxiety away, went to Adam, and said, "You and your father lent me this—gave it to me, actually. It's been really useful, but it doesn't exactly seem to fit very well lately. But thanks very much! It's really been very useful."

It is hard to give back a gift without sounding peevish or ungrateful, and I did not want to leave him with that impression of me. He was not paying much attention, as it happened, and said only, "Put it down over there, OK?" and went on with what he was doing.

One of my reasons for doing what I did was that talk was getting us nowhere; but all the same I felt a little let down. I had been prepared to defend my decision. And I thought that perhaps when he did notice he might be upset and want to talk. I put some things away and fiddled around a little, but he continued to do what he was doing and to take no notice of anything else. At last I said, "Well, goodbye, dear. I hope the garden key turns up."

He was fitting parts together, and said without looking around, "OK, fine, dear. When's dinner?"

"I'm not sure," I said. "I'm going now. With the—" I hesitated, and finally said, "With them, you know," and went on. In fact I had only just then realized how hard it would have been to explain myself. I could not chatter away as I used to do, taking it all for granted. My words now must be as slow, as new, as single, as tentative as the steps I took going down the path away from the house, between the dark-branched, tall dancers motionless against the winter shining.

(1985)